"After what happened last night—"

"What the hell happened last night?" Nathan swore before continuing. "I spent a half hour on the beach, letting you make a damn fool out of me, and then, following your directions, I walked dumbly into your mother's bedroom. What do you think happened then? Did she tell you I flung her on the bed and had my evil way with her?"

"No!"

"You surprise me."

"Don't you dare speak about my mother like that."

"Why not?" Nathan was too angry to be tactful. "Believe me, India, I've got nothing to thank that woman for."

ANNE MATHER **began her career by writing the kind of book she likes to read—romance. Married, with two children, this author from the north of England has become a favorite with readers of romance fiction the world over—her books have been translated into many languages and are read in countless countries. Anne enjoys reading, driving and traveling to new places to find settings for her novels.**

Books by Anne Mather

STORMSPELL
WILD CONCERTO
HIDDEN IN THE FLAME
THE LONGEST PLEASURE

HARLEQUIN PRESENTS PLUS

1567—RICH AS SIN
1591—TIDEWATER SEDUCTION

HARLEQUIN PRESENTS

1354—INDISCRETION
1444—BLIND PASSION
1458—SUCH SWEET POISON
1492—BETRAYED
1514—DIAMOND FIRE
1542—GUILTY
1553—DANGEROUS SANCTUARY
1617—SNOWFIRE

ANNE MATHER

Tender Assault

Harlequin Books

TORONTO • NEW YORK • LONDON
AMSTERDAM • PARIS • SYDNEY • HAMBURG
STOCKHOLM • ATHENS • TOKYO • MILAN
MADRID • WARSAW • BUDAPEST • AUCKLAND

ISBN 0-373-11649-7

TENDER ASSAULT

This edition published by arrangement with Harlequin Enterprises B. V.

Printed in U.S.A.

CHAPTER ONE

THE Cessna had been waiting for him when he landed at Nassau. He hadn't been sure it would be, but when he walked through Customs an unfamiliar face was waiting, holding a strip of cardboard with his name on it. He wondered why Sam Nevis hadn't come to meet him. The pilot his father had employed for the past twenty years was surely not old enough to be retired. But he knew nothing about his father's affairs any more, he reminded himself. And Sam Nevis, like everyone else, was just a name culled from the past.

The plane was unfamiliar, too, he found. The old single-engined turbo-prop had been replaced by a sleek, twin-engined jet, with all the comforts expected of such a sophisticated machine. Of course, it was the guests' first taste of the luxuries they could expect on Pelican Island, he conceded, and as such it had to be updated to meet an increasingly demanding clientele.

Or so he assumed, as he settled into one of the velvet armchairs that passed for aircraft seats. But, having read the island's publicity handouts in places as far apart as London and Sydney, New York and Tokyo, it was a fairly educated assumption. He had even felt a reluctant admiration for his father's enterprise, although he had suspected that Adele had been the driving force.

His lips twisted. How ironic, then, that all she had worked for should now be in jeopardy. How must she be feeling, knowing that the man she had tried to destroy was now capable of destroying her world? It was the ultimate humiliation. And, for the life of him, he couldn't understand why his father should have done such a thing. Unless...

But it was useless speculating. He had enough on his plate as it was without trying to second-guess something that might, just conceivably, turn out to be a mistake. It was always possible that his father had made another will. And where did India feature in this crazy scheme of things?

God! He ran a weary hand through the unruly darkness of his hair. And, because he had repeated this action frequently on the flight from New York, he wasn't surprised to find it was a mess. Besides, it needed cutting—had needed cutting since before his last trip to England. No wonder the Cessna's pilot had given him such a studied look when he'd turned up at the airport. In a worn Oxford shirt and jeans, and scuffed trainers, he was hardly the usual kind of guest welcomed at Kittrick's Hotel.

His palm scraped over his unshaven chin, and he grimaced. He supposed he should have waited, grabbed a night's sleep and a make-over, before presenting himself to his stepmother and his stepsister. He could have done it. His father was dead, for God's sake! The knowledge still pained him, but he ignored it. There was no earthly need for him to catch the next flight to the Bahamas, as if some almighty ruling was waiting on his arrival. He had all the time in the world to claim an inheritance he still couldn't believe was his. But when he had got back from Canada and found the cable waiting, giving himself time to think had not been on his agenda.

He gazed out of the window, wondering why it was that even after all these years he still felt such a knee-jerk reaction whenever he thought of home. It wasn't as if it had been his home for the past eight years. His father had kicked him out, for God's sake! He shouldn't forget that. And India had believed every word her mother had said. So why should he feel any emotion about going back? He wasn't even sure he wanted to do it, not deep down inside him.

But—and it was a big but—the present circumstances demanded that he at least should show his face. After all, it wasn't every day he had a multi-million-dollar holiday resort dropped in his lap. Forget the fact that there were probably lawyers and accountants, public relations consultants and managers to handle all the day-to-day problems of the hotel and island complex. This had been his father's creation. And, until he was twenty-one, he had shared it with him...

He grimaced. The tragedy was that he had never even known his father was ill. And he had been out of the country—and out of reach—when the news of the old man's death had been reported. In spite of everything, he would have liked to attend the funeral. And he would had done it, too, with or without Adele's and India's consent.

Of course, they probably wouldn't believe him. Or Adele might, but she'd make damn sure India didn't. Right now, she was doubtless poisoning his stepsister's mind with her version of why he was coming to the island. He hadn't bothered to come before, she'd say. But now, when there was money involved—an immense amount of money, if the publicity was to be believed—he was coming to collect, like the vulture he was.

A bitter smile tugged at the corners of his mouth. Well, in that respect, he could disabuse them—if he chose. He might have left the island without a penny, but he wasn't coming back that way. He had his own money now, his own thriving organisation, which he continued to control simply because he wanted to do so. He was no longer the cocky teenager he had been when his father had married for the second time. He was a man who knew the meaning of survival.

And that was what he had learned to do, in those first three years after he had left the island. He had joined the army, and any lingering traces of the boy he had once been had been sweated out of him in the jungles and rivers of Central America. But it had been a good training; it had instilled in him a respect of self-discipline that had given him the will, and the energy, to work for what he wanted.

When he left the army, he had had only the germ of an idea of what he wanted to do with the rest of his life. So he had gone to work at a summer camp, and in the variety of activities offered to the children he had seen the way to realise his ambitions.

He had decided to create a camp for adults, women as well as men, where, added to the usual fitness regime, he would offer the kind of experience previously only found within a military framework. Oh, he'd known it had to be provided within a comfortable ambience. The iron fist in the velvet glove. He had needed spa baths and saunas, expert masseurs to ease away the rigours of the day, and all the usual luxuries of hydrotherapy. His dream had been to create a kind of club where every physical need could be catered for. Somewhere where wives could learn tennis, and indulge in the most sinful forms of face and body massage, while their husbands climbed rocks, or white-water rafted, or battered their soft bodies into submission in some other macho pursuit.

Of course, he had known there would be women who wanted to go rock-climbing and men who wanted to play racket sports and be pampered, but he'd been prepared for all of that. The lodges he'd envisaged his guests staying in would be so comfortable that they'd be totally asexual. It would be a total resort, and sufficiently expensive so that only truly committed health freaks would come.

He had used the pay he had accumulated during his three years in the army to open his first camp. Most of his fellow rookies had spent their pay on beer and women, not necessarily in that order, but, apart from an initial phase of drunkenness, he had studiously saved his money. Besides, he had never had to pay for a woman in his life. Something about his heavy-lidded eyes and sun-burned features attracted females like a magnet. But it wasn't something he was proud of. Experience had taught him it was safer to stay away from the opposite sex.

Nevertheless, it had been a gamble, using every penny he had, plus a sizeable chunk of the bank's money, to buy a run-down fruit farm in Florida. And it had taken months of work to get the place anything like ready for his guests. But, because he had initially concentrated on the less usual activities offered by his establishment, he had attracted the media's attention, and in no time at all he was inundated by men desperate to escape from the confines of offices and boardrooms.

It was around this time that he had run into Greg Sanders again. Sanders had been his old drill sergeant, and in his early days at Fort Cleary he had hated the seemingly ruthless black officer. Sanders had picked on him relentlessly, and he had spent more time on the parade ground and worn out more boots than any of his fellow recruits.

Yet, in time, a genuine respect had grown between the two men, and, if in those early days they had never become friends, they had at least come to understand one another. And he knew that without Sanders's training he might never have survived those months in the jungle. He had been soft; he could admit it now. Being Aaron Kittrick's son had not prepared him for any other kind of life.

Consequently, when he learned that Sanders had retired from the army and was looking for work, he had been more than willing to offer the man a job. If anyone could lick his visitors into shape, Sanders could, and it was good to have someone working with him who was more than just an employee.

Sullivan's Spas took off. He had used his mother's maiden name, instead of his father's, so that no one could accuse him of trading on his father's reputation. Besides, it also gave him the anonymity he craved, and enabled him to move freely, without fear of recognition.

No one, least of all himself, could have imagined the spas' success. From that small beginning, they had mushroomed all across the United States. And, because most health clubs were in urban areas, and he had concentrated on creating his resorts in less civilised surroundings, there was the added novelty of communing with nature, of seeing birds and animals in their natural habitat.

Besides, he knew that his spas were in some of the most beautiful country in the world: Southern California; Colorado; South Dakota; New Mexico; not to mention the pioneer resort in Florida, and other establishments all along the eastern seaboard. He had been lucky, in that land in the places he wanted to expand was not expensive. In consequence, he could afford to build low and consider the environment.

Over the years, Greg Sanders had trained a score of instructors, who now worked under him. He no longer worked in the field himself, although they both spent periodic sabbaticals at each and every spa, making sure they were running smoothly, and that their guests were happy. On Greg's fiftieth birthday, he had actually given him a quarter share of the business, making him the chief shareholder, aside from himself.

And it was because of his company that he had been out of the country—and out of reach—when his father died. He had been in a mountainous district of British Columbia, researching the possibilities of opening a new resort in that most remote part of Canada. The only way in had been by float-plane and canoe, and it had teased his interest speculating the incongruity of creating an oasis of luxury in such primitive surroundings. Of course, it would have to be carefully planned, as such projects always were. He could now afford to employ the best brains in the world, and if another Sullivan Spa was built it would blend expertly into the scenery. Log cabins, he thought, raw on the outside, but offering every conceivable luxury within. And pools fed by filtered lake-water, icy cold or steaming . . .

The short flight was almost over. The stewardess, who had offered him a drink after boarding, now appeared to ask him to fasten his seatbelt for landing. Like the pilot, she had looked at him with enquiry in her eyes. But, unlike the pilot, there had been speculation in them, too.

He wondered whose idea it had been to have a stewardess on a flight that lasted less than half an hour. No doubt her short skirt and trim figure was much appreciated by any male visitors. But was the bodice of her scarlet tunic usually unbuttoned, so that the dusky hollow of her cleavage was distinctly visible as she bent to take his empty glass? And did she usually circle her glistening lips with her tongue as she removed the monogrammed coaster?

He decided not to theorise, though his expression was faintly cynical as he turned back to the small window. Maybe it was Adele's way of reminding him that she hadn't forgotten—or forgiven him, for not wanting her. Perhaps it was intended to arouse his libido, to taunt him with memories of what he had rejected.

Or maybe he was just too sensitive, he reflected wryly. And sensitivity, in any form, was not what was needed here. Incredible as it seemed, his father had made him his only heir. Kittrick's Hotel, Pelican Island; it was all his now. And, however, Adele chose to play it, he was in command.

The small jet was making its approach to the island now, and, dismissing his thoughts, he took a concentrated look at the place that had been his home for more than fifteen years. His father had bought Pelican Island with the idea of creating a private resort for deep-sea fishermen, yachtsmen and the like, and by the time he was sixteen it had become a thriving little business. Guests shared rooms in the sprawling plantation house that had been their home in those days, and, although the accommodation was fairly basic, no one seemed to mind. He remembered his schooldays as being long days spent crewing the thirty-foot schooner his father charted out to would-be anglers, and hot nights on the beach, eating barbecued grouper, and talking about the big marlin or barracuda that just got away.

Until Adele came on the scene, he brooded. Adele and her seven-year-old daughter, India. Adele, with her big ideas about building a proper hotel and expanding the facilities they could offer. Adele, who had met his father on one of his infrequent trips to London to visit his late wife's mother, and who had seen in Aaron Kittrick the promise of a financially secure future.

His long fingers combed impatiently through his hair again. His assessment of Adele's motives was harsh, and he knew it. But it was also accurate. From the very beginning, he had seen right through the girlish façade she had adopted for his father's benefit. The wonder was that his father hadn't been able to see through it, too. But, from being a mild-mannered man who had always had time for his son—even when that son had tried his patience considerably—he had changed into a lovesick schoolboy with little or no interest in anything his son had to say. He had been infatuated with Adele, bewitched by her doll-like beauty, flattered that a woman with such obvious sex appeal should be attracted to a man undoubtedly past the emotive watershed of middle age.

The only advantage he had gained from this unlikely pairing was India. Although he hadn't realised it at first. At fifteen, he had had little time for the skinny kid who dogged his footsteps. She was a nuisance, and he'd lost no time in telling her so.

But India hadn't taken offence. And, as time went by, and she had showed no signs of taking advantage of her position, he had softened. Besides, it had actually been quite a novelty, having a stepsister. He had always been an only child, and in the years between his father's marriage to Adele and his graduation he and India had become good friends.

In some ways she had been old for her years—due in part to Adele's neglect, he reflected—and she had been quite content to sit for hours, listening to him expound on every subject under the sun. She had been good for his ego, he acknowledged, and, as Adele had persuaded Aaron to invest in building a new hotel, and he and his father had become more and more alienated, India had been the recipient of all his boyish frustrations.

On the more positive side, he had taught her to swim and snorkel. He'd taken her to explore the wonders of the reef that lay to the east of Pelican Island. He'd shown her how to dive for clams, and given her a guided tour of all the secret coves he had discovered throughout the lonely years of his childhood. During his holidays they had been inseparable, and he had started treating her as an equal, as well as a friend.

Until Adele had intervened. She had never liked their relationship. Looking back, he wondered if she had been jealous, but even now that interpretation of her behaviour stuck in his throat. What possible reason could she have had to be jealous of a schoolgirl?

Whatever, she had ultimately succeeded in parting them. That final summer vacation, when matters had come to a head, she had successfully driven a wedge between them. She had told India, in his and his father's hearing, that she had to stop bothering him. She had said he had told her he was sick of India, that for the past six years he had put up with her, but now it had to stop, that he was a man, not a boy, and the last thing he needed was some overweight, spotty teenager like her cramping his style.

Of course, he had denied it, but he had seen the uncertainty in India's face. And, when his father had asked him outright if he was calling Adele a liar, he had backed down. It had been a cowardly thing to do, he knew, and he had played right into Adele's hands. But in a choice between rowing with his father or hurting India, there had been no contest. And he had still been young enough—and naïve enough—to believe the alienation from his father was not already irrevocable...

The Cessna banked steeply, and he looked out on the palm-strewn beaches of his youth. A curving sweep of coral sand fringed an ocean that paled from deepest blue to the clearest turquoise, with banks of seaweed submerged and moving in the current. Pelican Island, he thought, was no longer just an angler's paradise, but one of the most exclusive resorts in the world.

The landing-strip seemed to come rushing up to meet them, and the powerful little jet squealed across the concrete. Windermere Bay; Cat Point; Abalone Cove; all the names he had once known so well came surging back to greet him. For the first time in more than eight years, he was coming home.

He wondered who they would send to meet him. It was nearly three miles from the airport at Green Turtle Hill to the hotel at Abaco Beach. In his day, guests had been transported over the last few miles of their journey in one of the minibuses that had been used as well for tours around the island. But that was before Kittrick's Hotel had received its five-star status. These days, they probably used Rolls-Royces or Cadillacs to ferry their guests around.

The plane had stopped next to a white-painted building that served as both immigration area and traffic control. All guests were registered as they arrived on the island, and he was relieved to see that, apart from a coat of paint, the place looked little different from what he remembered.

'I hope you enjoyed the trip, Mr Kittrick,' the stewardess said, after the door of the aircraft had been opened, and the flight of steps unfolded. 'Have a nice day!'

'Thanks.'

But as he shook hands with the pilot, he noticed her tunic was now sedately buttoned. Perhaps she had been acting on her own behalf, her reflected drily. They all must know that he was the new owner of Pelican Island. And it was his own fault for dressing so casually, and maybe allowing her to think he might be flattered by a little healthy provocation. New owners sometimes meant new staff, and it was incredible to think he had the last word on her employment. He could almost feel sympathy for the core of her dilemma.

But experience had taught him that nothing came for free, and, hefting his overnight bag, he descended the steps without looking back. God, the sun was hot, he thought, feeling the tight jeans sticking to him like a second skin. He should have changed on the plane. He had some shorts in his bag. But he had been too preoccupied with his thoughts to give any real consideration to the climate.

He stood for a moment at the foot of the aircraft's steps, gazing about him. There was always a breeze on the island, which moderated the heat and made the temperature so delightful. And it was particularly evident here on Green Turtle Hill, a warm breeze that lifted his hair from his sweat-dampened neck and plastered his shirt against his body.

'Nathan.'

He hadn't been aware of anyone's approach. He had been staring at the sun-bleached air-strip, at the fluttering tops of the flame-trees and at the lush vegetation that sloped away towards the beach. His eyes had settled on the ocean cresting like lace upon the sand, and his ears had been filled with its muted thunder as it splintered on the reef.

But now his gaze was drawn to the young woman standing patiently beside him, a tall, slim, striking woman, with cool, sculptured features and long straight hair that was presently caught back with an elastic band. Her eyes were blue, her nose was straight, and her mouth was full and generous. But it was the brilliance of her hair that gave her away, the glorious fall of bright red silk, and the delicate pale skin that went with it.

'India?' he said, half incredulously, and her mouth tightened almost imperceptibly.

'Nathan,' she repeated. 'Welcome home. I'm sorry it's in such unhappy circumstances.'

'Yes.' Nathan couldn't get over the change in her. When he had gone away, India had been five feet two at most, and, although she hadn't deserved her mother's description of her as being overweight and spotty, she had been suffering the usual pains of adolescence. 'I'm sorry, too.' He paused. 'It's good to see you again, India.'

Her smile was perfunctory. 'Shall we go?' she suggested. She glanced at his canvas holdall before gesturing towards the back of the building. 'The buggy's just over there.' She turned to the pilot, who had been observing their reunion. 'Raoul, will you fetch the rest of Mr Kittrick's luggage off the plane?'

'No,' Nathan intervened before the pilot could speak. 'That is—I don't have any more luggage.' He tapped the canvas holdall. 'This is it.'

India's brows, which were several shades darker than her hair, drew together in obvious confusion. 'You mean—it's coming on later,' she said, evidently not enjoying having her arrangements thwarted in front of the staff, and Nathan shook his head.

'I've got everything I need,' he assured her smoothly. He gave the pilot and his companion a faintly mocking salute. 'Thanks, Raoul. It was a very—enjoyable trip.'

He didn't look at the stewardess, but he guessed she was relieved he hadn't chosen to mention her. All the same, it made him wonder about the kind of stories that were circulating about him. What kind of man did they think he was? What other lies had Adele been spreading since she had learned she was not to inherit Pelican Island after all?

He felt a surge of irritation, not least because he didn't like the idea of India hearing that her stepbrother was some sort of sex animal. She might already think it, of course. Goodness knew, she had been brainwashed into believing he had no scruples. He wasn't a monk, and he'd never pretended to be one. But he'd spent most of his energies these past years in making a success of his business, not feeding his libido.

'Oh, well . . .' India lifted her slim shoulders in a dismissing motion, and started towards the black- and white-painted buggy parked in the shade of the building. 'Let's go.'

Nathan took a moment to observe the spectacle of her trim rear, tightly encased in black close-fitting shorts, before following her. He already knew her breasts were full and round and strained against the white silk of the vest that completed her outfit. The shadow of her bra had been clearly visible as he'd looked down at her, and he guessed she was one of the hotel's less obvious assets.

This thought irritated him, also. He didn't like the image of some rich banker feasting his eyes on India's slender body. She was his sister, for God's sake! He didn't want anyone looking at her but him. He knew a sudden urge to protect her. Was Adele exploiting her daughter, as well as everything else?

India was sitting in the buggy when he reached it, her hands on the wheel, and the motor running. Nathan tossed his bag into the back, and swung himself into the seat beside her. 'Right,' he said, giving her a brooding sideways glance, and she put the gearstick into drive, and pressed her booted foot on the accelerator.

The road had been much improved, he noticed at once. The rutted track he remembered had been repaired and edged with coral, but it was an ongoing problem. It was impossible to control all the vegetation on the island, and trailing vines hid the road in places. On top of that, grass was pushing up among the coral, and here and there the heads of periwinkles nodded as they passed. There was a glorious inconsistency about the landscaping here, he thought ruefully. Tropical shrubs grew in the most unlikely places, and, despite the frustration, their beauty was unsurpassed.

'Did you have a good flight?'

Her question took him by surprise, and he had to check the urge to ask her if she cared. Her attitude towards him—polite, but superficial—was not what he'd anticipated, not what he *wanted*. Didn't she feel any emotion, for God's sake? He'd expected anger, or resentment, but not indifference.

But it was too soon to voice his feelings. Particularly as he wasn't entirely sure what those feelings were. At the moment, he was still assimilating his reaction to her appearance, reminding himself that this was the wide-eyed kid who'd once hung on his every word.

So, 'Pretty good,' he responded, half turning in his seat towards her, and resting one arm along the back of hers. He hesitated, and then, 'How's your mother? Was she here when the old man bought—er—died?'

'Of course she was here.' With the first flash of spirit he had seen, India answered him. 'He'd been ill for several weeks. The local doctor thought it was just overwork. He wouldn't go to see a specialist. He was having some pain, you see, and he insisted it was just a pulled muscle.'

Nathan felt an unwilling tightness in his throat. 'But it wasn't.'

'No.' India shook her head and a silky strand of her long hair brushed his knuckles. 'Afterwards—after the heart attack that killed him—they discovered a small embolism in his chest. It—was very quick.'

Nathan turned his hand and captured the fiery thread, smoothing it between his fingers. 'I see.'

'We did try to reach you,' she added. 'But we didn't know where you were living. Fortunately, Mr Hastings——' his father's lawyer, he remembered '—located an address in New York. But, as you know, you weren't there.'

'No.' She moved her head again and he let go of her hair. 'I was—out of the country. Still——' his lips twisted '—I doubt if I was missed.'

Her eyes turned to him then, cool and dispassionate. 'You are his son,' she said, as if that was enough, and the rawness of injustice stirred inside him.

'Not for the past eight years,' he said, baring his resentment. 'The old man threw me off the island, if you remember. I didn't get the impression he ever wanted me back.'

India's fingers tightened on the steering-wheel, and for a few moments she said nothing, allowing him to draw his own conclusions. But it was difficult to sustain any bitterness here, with the spicy scents of the island invading his nostrils, and the lowering sun touching everything with a golden brilliance. He'd forgotten exactly how beautiful it all was, and he gazed at the drooping heads of mimosa and oleander with an equal measure of ambivalence.

The road was dipping down towards the shoreline, and, to their left, the manicured lawns of a golf course defied the hand of nature. Beyond the trunk of a flowering jacaranda, he could see the coral roof of the clubhouse, and the gaily painted carts that ferried the guests around.

Evidently Adele had been busy, he reflected wryly, remembering this area as being a flowering wilderness. But these days no resort worth its salt could do without a golf course, and even a desultory glance disclosed that this was a rather better one than most.

'He never stopped loving you, you know,' India said suddenly, into the faintly hostile silence that had fallen, and Nathan gave her a searching look.

'No?' He was sceptical.

'No.' She clung to the wheel as the buggy bounced over a wooden bridge that arched a small ravine. 'He used to talk about you a lot.' She paused. 'Particularly towards—towards the end.'

Nathan's jaw compressed. What was he supposed to say to that? What was he supposed to think? Did she think it comforted him to believe his father had forgiven him? Dammit; as far as he was concerned, there was nothing to forgive.

'And what about you?' he asked, somewhat mockingly, eager to change the subject, and she gave him a startled glance.

'What about me?'

'Do you still love me?' he asked, wanting to disconcert her, and a feathering of colour brushed her skin.

She had beautiful skin, he noticed, pale and delicate, but with the rich lushness of cream. She had never tanned, but she had also escaped the bane of freckles that many redheads suffered. Instead, her arms and legs were smooth and unblemished, and disturbingly appealing.

'Of course,' she said at once, her reply swift and defensive, and he found himself staring at her, resenting her generosity. How could she love someone who, if she believed her mother, had despised and insulted her? Someone, moreover, who had betrayed them all, particularly his father? But, 'You're my brother,' she added simply, and Nathan felt as if someone had just kicked him in the gut...

CHAPTER TWO

'So where is he?'

Adele Kittrick turned from applying a moisturising foundation to her face and neck, and regarded her daughter impatiently. In a coral silk wrapper, with her skilfully bleached hair hidden beneath a black turban, she looked rather more than the forty-two years she admitted to. It didn't help that her expression was taut and demanding. India was the only person who ever saw her mother at her worst.

'He said he was going to take a shower,' India replied now, hooking her hip over the arm of a satin-striped *chaise-longue*, and meeting her mother's gaze without rancour. 'I've put him in 204, as we decided. If I'd known you wanted me to bring him here, I'd have made other arrangements.'

'I didn't want you to bring him here,' retorted her mother shortly, turning back to survey her reflection in the mirror of the dressing-table. 'I just find it hard to believe that he didn't mention the will as you were driving back from the airport. It must be on his mind, for God's sake. It's why he's come here. To make fools of us all!'

India drew her lower lip between her teeth. 'I don't think you can blame Nathan for what his father did,' she said cautiously. 'He knew nothing about the will. And he certainly didn't influence Daddy.'

'How do you know that?' Adele screwed the cap back on to the jar of cream and slammed it down on the tray in front of her. The crystal rang protestingly, but fortunately it didn't shatter. Nevertheless, India's nails curled into her palms at this obvious display of temper.

'Mother, you know Daddy hasn't spoken to Nathan for over eight years,' her daughter replied steadily. 'Why, even Mr Hastings didn't have his address.'

Adele snorted. 'Oh, yes, go on. Defend him, India. You always did. Even though you knew what he'd said about you, how he'd treated you, you still ran around after him like a lovesick puppy!'

India drew a calming breath. This was an old argument, and one she had learned not to pursue. It used to hurt—it might still hurt, if she let it. But she knew it was just her mother's way of expunging her frustration, of letting out some of the bitterness that was eating her up.

'Well, what did you talk about, then?' Adele persisted now, when it became apparent that her previous taunt was not about to bear fruit. 'Is he still as arrogant as ever—as aggressive? What?'

India carefully uncurled her fingers and smoothed them over the expanded Lycra of her shorts. She was glad her mother was looking at her own reflection at that moment, and not at her. But that didn't prevent her palms from growing moist, or stop a trickle of sweat from running down between her breasts.

'He's—older,' she said at last, realising that was hardly a satisfactory response, but needing to say something before her mother became suspicious of her silence. 'And—he's very brown. I'd say that, whatever he's been doing for the past eight years, it hasn't been in an office.'

Adele's eyes shifted to her daughter's face. 'Well, what did you expect?' she demanded scathingly, and India was so relieved she had noticed nothing amiss that she didn't voice any protest. 'He's probably been herding cattle or working on an oil rig! God knows, he wasn't fit for anything else. When I think of how we've worked to make a success of this place, I could weep. It's just not fair that he should get it all.'

'No.' India had to concede her mother's final point at least. But Nathan was his father's flesh and blood. She had only ever been second-best.

Adele picked up a tube of lip-gloss, and examined the colour intently. 'Did—er—did he ask about me?' she enquired, and, although India had been expecting the question, it still caught her unawares.

'He—asked how you were,' she admitted honestly, managing to contain the wave of heat that threatened to invade her neck. And then, rushing on, 'But mostly he talked about Daddy. He wanted to know the details of how he died.'

Adele's mouth took on a sullen twist. 'As if he cared,' she exclaimed malevolently. 'I hope you told him his father never spoke of him. I don't remember Aaron even mentioning his name in my hearing.'

India got abruptly to her feet. That wasn't true, but she knew better than to say so. 'I'd better go,' she said, aware that, for all her apparent composure, she couldn't take much more. It hadn't been an easy day for her either, and even her cultivated detachment was wearing dangerously thin. 'I promised Carlos I'd speak to Paolo about serving drinks while he's playing. And I've got to get changed yet. I'm supposed to be having dinner with Senator Markham and his wife.'

Adele grimaced. 'He won't expect you to keep to that arrangement, India. Besides, it was business, wasn't it? Why should you continue to take bookings when, as far as we know, Nathan could boot us out tomorrow?'

India breathed out slowly. 'I—don't think he'll do that, Mother.'

'How do you know? Has he said so?'

'No——'

'There you are, then.' Adele sighed with frustration. 'I wish you'd stop thinking that you know him better than I do. He's a rat, India. A bastard! He's totally without scruples, and you'd better start believing it!'

She did!

As India made some perfunctory comment about not having time to discuss Nathan now, and left her mother's room, her nerves were working overtime. And, with the door closed behind her, she took a moment to get herself back together. But her mother's words were far too potent to dismiss that easily, and the fact that they were true made them impossible to forget.

Nathan was everything her mother had said. He had behaved abominably, and had almost broken his father's heart. It had taken Aaron Kittrick years to get over what his son had done, and her mother had borne the brunt of the depression he had suffered because of it.

Squaring her shoulders, India determinedly put that memory behind her. However Nathan had behaved, whatever he had done, it was pointless thinking about it now. Evidently his father had forgiven him, or he would not have made him his heir. It was no use her feeling bitter. Her mother was nursing enough bitterness for both of them.

The family apartments were situated in a separate wing of the hotel. Connected to the main building by means of a vine-hung colonnade, it was a single-storey dwelling, with a pink-tiled hipped roof, and long windows, opening on to a paved terrace. It was sufficiently apart from the other hotel buildings to ensure complete privacy, but near enough so that any problems could be dealt with at once. After all, it was the very personal service they offered that had made Kittrick's Hotel and Pelican Island world-famous. It prided itself on its reputation for providing both comfort and individuality, and, although it had accommodated many visitors over the years, a careful record was kept of each guest's likes and dislikes.

Of course, it helped that the hotel could only accommodate a maximum of thirty guests at any one time. Eighteen suites catered to the needs of visitors as diverse as politicians and pop stars, their exclusivity ensuring that if privacy was sought it would be found. There were no sensation seekers on Pelican Island, no publicity hounds, no fans wanting autographs. Indeed, there were times when the whole hotel was filled with a single party, and it wasn't uncommon for an anonymous guest to turn out to be a very familiar face.

It was almost dark as India entered the cathedral-like foyer of the hotel. But the enormous chandelier suspended from the cavernous ceiling cast its mellow glow over the many plants and floral displays that gave the huge reception area a colourful ambience. As well as the chandelier, a sprinkling of lamps, set beside groupings of chairs and sofas, created small oases of intimacy and comfort, while the stripped pine floor was strewn with Chinese rugs, thick and rich and delicately patterned.

There were few people about at this hour of the evening. From experience, India knew that most guests were either bathing or resting at this time, or enjoying a rejuvenating massage from one of the hotel's team of health therapists. After a day spent swimming, or sailing, or simply soaking up the sun, it was good to relax and be pampered. Kittrick's Hotel was equipped with every device necessary to make their guests happy, and men, as well as women, took advantage of its many facilities.

It was later that the bar would fill up and the poolside restaurant would start serving the score of gourmet delicacies cooked up by their French chef and his expert staff. But for now the public rooms were practically deserted, except for the ever present army of stewards, some of whom were always on duty.

Nevertheless, India felt slightly under-dressed as she crossed to the reception desk. By this time, she was usually changed for the evening, and although her presence wasn't always necessary, she preferred to keep an eye on things. But Nathan's arrival had upset the normal scheme of things, and she was still struggling to come to terms with her own reaction to it.

'Oh, hello, Miss Kittrick.' The receptionist left the pile of credit slips she had been systematically entering into the computer, and came to greet her. 'Is something wrong?'

'What?' For a moment, India wondered if she meant Nathan, and then, realising it was her appearance that had produced such a comment, she shook her head. 'Oh—no. No.' She forced a smile. 'I just wanted to have a word with Paolo. Do you know where he is?'

'He's in the bar, Miss Kittrick,' said the girl at once. 'Your—er—brother wanted a drink.' She paused. 'He's very nice, isn't he? Your brother, I mean. So—easy-going and friendly. Not—not at all like... well, like his father, is he?'

She was embarrassed and showed it, but, having started the sentence, she had had to finish it. India sympathised with her. And it was true, she thought unwillingly. In latter years, Nathan's father had become more and more remote. India had put his uncertain moods down to his health. There was no denying that, for the past eighteen months at least, Aaron Kittrick had not been a well man. He had been withdrawn and unsociable, even with her. But now she was not so sure of her conclusion. Had his estrangement from Nathan been preying on his mind? she wondered. She would probably never know.

But, more immediately, she had the unenviable prospect of facing Nathan again, if she wanted to speak to Paolo before the evening's entertainment began. She would have preferred to avoid seeing Nathan, at least until she had had time to bathe and change. Without the armour of clothes and make-up she felt absurdly vulnerable, a circumstance for which Nathan was wholly responsible.

He had embarrassed her horribly that afternoon by asking her that unforgivable question. And she had made it worse by admitting that she still cared about him. She should have evaded an answer, made some glib response that wouldn't commit her either way. Instead, she had been so desperate to prove her own detachment that she had laid herself open to the kind of ridicule he could so readily produce.

Once it wouldn't have bothered her. She had grown up with his teasing, and she'd always believed it was without malice. Until her mother had pointed out how unsuitable it was for a thirteen-year-old to go on treating Nathan as her contemporary. Until she had made it plain that he was just too polite to tell her to get lost.

India remembered how humiliated she had felt when she'd realised that truth. She had followed Nathan everywhere, it was true, but she'd never had a brother before, especially not an older brother who could do all the things she herself was desperate to learn.

She'd thought he'd enjoyed her company, too, and perhaps he had, to begin with. Perhaps, like her, he'd found having a ready-made sibling quite appealing. Particularly one who admired him, and hung on his every word.

But there was an enormous difference between the hero-worship of a seven-year-old and the embarrassing persistence of a post-pubescent teenager. And, as soon as her mother remarked on it, India had known she must be right. Of course then she hadn't realised where his desires lay, hadn't understood that his tolerance with her had just been a means to an end...

Now she straightened her spine, made a reassuring remark to the red-faced receptionist, and walked determinedly across the foyer. She couldn't blame the girl for responding to Nathan's charm. She knew only too well how lethal that charm could be.

The cocktail bar was four steps down from the level of the foyer. Cool and dim, with a long counter strung with lights, it overlooked the beach, and the lights of the marina in the distance. Her stepfather had built the marina in the days before Kittrick's Hotel had become a household name. The old house, where they had lived when she and her mother had first come here, had been both hotel and residence. However, since the new hotel had been constructed, it had been turned into a haven for yachtsmen. There was a clubhouse now, on the upper floor, and a comprehensive chandlery beneath. And, although the store was supposed to be there for the benefit of the yachting community, it also sold golf and scuba-diving gear, and female guests could often be found browsing through its racks of designer sportswear, or chatting up the manager, who was, admittedly, quite a hunk.

India halted at the top of the steps leading down into the bar, and surveyed the territory. The piano where Carlos Mendoza played most evenings was as yet unattended, and there were no couples smooching on the tiny dance-floor. The neat armchairs and tables that were set by the long windows to take advantage of the view were still empty, and the distant sounds from the stereo were soft and not intrusive.

She saw Nathan at once, seated on one of the tall stools at the bar, talking to Paolo. And why wouldn't she? she asked herself impatiently. Apart from the bartender, he was the only occupant. Nevertheless, it was galling to feel her pulses racing, and she thrust aside the feeling that he had already taken control.

He had changed, she noticed. The well-worn jeans that had clung to his muscled thighs had given way to black chinos and a dark shirt. His dark hair overhung his collar at the back, and even from here she could see it was still damp from his shower. But, when Paolo suddenly noticed her, and said something to his companion, Nathan turned his head in her direction, and she focused on the fact that the tie they insisted upon was absent.

All the same, it was a little unnerving to have him watch her descend the steps and cross the polished floor towards them. She was intensely conscious of her windswept hair and bare arms and legs, and she prayed she wouldn't trip or do something equally stupid.

'Hi,' he said when she reached them, and she was glad he didn't slide off the bar-stool to greet her. As it was, with his arms on the counter, and his shoulders hunched over the Scotch and water in front of him, he was almost her own height, and she didn't experience the same lack of advantage she'd felt at the airport.

'Hello,' she responded, managing a smile, even if it was a trifle chilly. But Nathan disturbed her, and she didn't like the sensation. She was letting his lack of sensitivity get to her, and she knew she would have to deal with it.

'You look harassed,' he remarked, and she thought how typical it was of him to make such a personal comment. She knew how she looked. She didn't need him to tell her. And, when it came right down to it, it was none of his business, so why didn't he butt out?

'You don't,' she remarked now, noticing he had shaved the growth of stubble from his chin. It didn't make him look any younger; it just accentuated the harsh beauty of his features.

'Is that supposed to mean something?' he enquired, rubbing his nose with a lazy finger. His eyes were lazy, too, dark and inscrutable behind their shield of sooty lashes.

'I—we—guests are expected to wear a tie in the evening,' she explained, not without some trepidation. She could tell herself that this was her stepbrother, that it was Nathan, with whom she had once shared all her girlish confidences, but it didn't work. Too much had happened. He had gone away and they had grown apart. The man he was now bore little resemblance to the boy she remembered.

'Really?'

Nathan's fingers probed the open collar of his shirt, which she could now see was made of navy blue silk. So wherever he had been, and whatever he had done, he hadn't been penniless, she reflected tautly, trying to avoid watching those long narrow fingers as they exposed the sun-burned column of his throat.

'Yes, really,' she confirmed, grateful that she sounded more resolute than she felt. Her gaze strayed to the faintly mocking curve of his mouth. 'I'm sorry.'

Nathan's lips parted, revealing teeth that were white and even. 'And that's the purpose of this visit?' he enquired. 'To tell me I'm not properly dressed?' His lips twisted. 'Forgive me, but are you saying that what you're wearing is suitable, but I'm out of line?'

'No!' India was impatient. 'No, of course not. I came to speak to Paolo. I didn't know I'd find you here, did I?'

Nathan inclined his head. 'Maybe not,' he conceded, raising his glass to his lips. 'So do you want me to leave you two alone?'

India refused to dignify his words with a reply. Instead she turned to Paolo, and, adopting the polite but authoritative manner she used with all the staff, she explained Carlos's predicament.

'He'd like you to avoid clattering glasses while he's playing,' she clarified carefully. 'Most people are prepared to wait until each medley's over before being served. And those who won't wait will come to the counter. Your moving round the room, taking orders, is distracting the guests while they're listening to the music.'

Paolo was scowling when she'd finished, and India suppressed a sigh. The Italian barman was not the easiest person to deal with, and he and Carlos had crossed swords before. 'What he means is he's afraid he won't get his tips if I give them something else to think about,' he retorted, in the hoarse accented English the women guests found so appealing. '*Dio*, doesn't the *idiota* realise that so far as the guests are concerned I might just as well be playing the stereo?'

'I don't think that's entirely true, Paolo,' she declared evenly. 'Carlos is a very accomplished musician——'

'*E puntura*!' grunted Paolo sulkily, and although India didn't know what that meant she was sure it was nothing complimentary.

'I don't think——' she was beginning wearily, when Nathan intervened.

'I think you owe Miss Kittrick an apology,' he said, his voice no less compelling because it was low and controlled. 'And if she tells you not to serve drinks while this pianist is doing his stuff you won't do it. Right?'

Paolo's reaction was immediate. 'But of course, *signore*,' he exclaimed, and if India hadn't already had experience of his belligerence she would have thought she had imagined it. 'I was only joking, no? Carlos—he is my friend. We are all friends here on Pelican Island.'

India's jaw compressed. It had not been a good day for her, and this was the last straw. It was bad enough that Nathan should have felt the need—or believed he had the *right*—to involve himself in her affairs, but Paolo's response was humiliating.

'As I was saying,' she continued, through her teeth, 'I don't think there is any advantage to be gained in insulting one another. Carlos has his job to do, just as you have yours. And I don't think I need to remind you that good bartenders are easier to find than good musicians. Do I make myself clear?'

Paolo cast a grudging glance at Nathan, as if gauging his reaction to her words, and then, with a shrug of his dinner-jacket-clad shoulders, he submitted. 'Yes, *signora*.'

'Good.' India permitted herself a taut look in her stepbrother's direction, and then pushed herself away from the counter. 'And now, if you'll excuse me——'

'Wait!'

She had reached the shallow steps leading up into the foyer when Nathan caught up with her. For a brief moment she had thought he was going to let her go without saying anything more, but she ought to have known better.

'Yes?' she said now, turning to face him with what she hoped was calm indifference.

'What was all that about?' he demanded, casting a meaningful look behind him. 'Why the cold shoulder?'

'I beg your pardon?' India pretended ignorance. She glanced at the slim gold watch on her wrist, the watch her stepfather had bought her for her twenty-first birthday, and frowned. 'I don't have time to talk now. I have to get changed.'

'That's not what I mean and you know it,' retorted Nathan flatly. 'What's the matter? Did I say something wrong?'

India stiffened. 'Why should you think that?'

'I didn't mistake that look you gave me just now,' he answered. 'It was lethal. Well, OK, if there's something you want to say to me, let's have it. I don't like innuendo; I never have.'

India took a deep breath. She didn't want to get into this. Not right now. She was hot, and she was tired, and the prospect of a cool shower was all she wanted to think about. 'You're imagining things,' she said, deciding there was no point in making a big thing of it. After all, Nathan owned the place now. If he chose to remonstrate with the staff, who was she to complain?

She would have turned away again, but Nathan's fingers curled about her arm, preventing her. 'I am not imagining things,' he said, with quiet force. 'I guess you didn't like me butting into your conversation with the barkeep. That's the only thing it can be, unless I said something this afternoon that's made you mad. Hell, tell me if it bugs you! I don't want there to be any misunderstandings between us.'

India swallowed, wondering why Nathan's hand was causing such a furious reaction inside her. Where those hard fingers touched, her skin felt as if it were on fire, and a hot stream of awareness was shooting up her arm. It was as if her whole body was focused on that careless grip, and she could hear her own heartbeat pounding in her ears.

She was over-reacting. She knew it. Heavens, it wasn't as if Nathan had never touched her before. In the days before her mother had made her aware of her own foolishness, he had often grabbed her arm to emphasise a point, or to drag her out to go fishing. Of all his activities, going fishing had been the one she liked least, and they had often done battle over who was to get their way. He even used to pick her up and throw her into the water sometimes, and she'd try to wrestle him underwater to get her own back. They'd been totally unselfconscious with each other in those days, so why was she getting so upset that it took every bit of determination she possessed not to tear herself away from him?

Realising there was only one way to deal with it, she tipped her chin towards him. 'I think you know what you did,' she declared, her tone clipped and aggressive. 'It might have slipped your notice, but the hotel's been running just fine while you've been away!'

Nathan's lips tightened. 'You thought I was interfering,' he stated evenly. 'So why didn't you just say so?'

India snorted. 'I thought I just did.'

'Not before I had to practically drag it out of you,' retorted Nathan. 'And while we're on the subject, why don't you let Adele do her own dirty work? If she wants the Italian put in his place, let her do it. You're not her lackey.'

India blinked, momentarily distracted from her efforts to avoid his dark, accusing gaze. 'Adele?' she echoed blankly. 'My mother? What's she got to do with this?'

Nathan frowned, his eyes searching her increasingly hot face. 'She does have the final say about what goes down, doesn't she?'

'What goes down?' India gave an impatient exclamation. 'I don't know what you're talking about.'

'All right.' Nathan's tone was considerably less friendly now. 'She may employ a manager—who may or may not be you, I don't know—but she signs the cheques, doesn't she? Or rather she did, when my father was alive.'

'No!' Now India did pull herself away from him. 'My mother's never taken any part in the running of the hotel. When Daddy...when your father was alive he trusted me to handle the practical side of it. My mother—she travels a lot. This is a small island. People get—restless.'

'Don't you mean bored?' suggested Nathan harshly, though he was evidently having some difficulty in coming to terms with what she had said. 'So... Kittrick's Hotel, Pelican Island—this was your baby?'

'I didn't say that.' India was defensive now. 'You know it was my mother's idea to expand the resort——'

'Because it wasn't earning enough money to satisfy her as it was,' put in Nathan caustically, but India chose to ignore him.

'And Daddy—that is, your father—arranged the finance.'

'You mean he put himself in hock to the bank?' Nathan's mouth curled. 'Oh, yes, I know about that.'

India took a deep breath. 'If you're going to persist in making rude remarks, then I don't think I want to go on with this,' she declared stiffly. 'I'm sure Mr Hastings must have given you all the details. If you need any more information, I suggest you ask him.'

'Ah—damn!'

Nathan swore volubly and colourfully, and India squared her shoulders and started up the steps. She had no reason to tolerate his crudeness, she told herself. She didn't have to defend herself to him, and she particularly didn't have to defend her mother.

'All right, all right, I'm sorry.' His unexpected apology came from behind her left ear, and she realised he had followed her out of the bar. He was now standing on the step immediately below her, which accounted for the fact that his breath was fanning her neck and not the top of her head. 'As far as Hastings is concerned,' he went on, 'he supplied all the necessary information, sure, but not the *details*. Dammit, I haven't even met with the guy. As soon as I read his cable, I came right here.'

India turned towards him with some reluctance. And, because he was lower than she was, their eyes were almost on a level. It meant she had no chance of avoiding his defensive stare, and she crossed her arms across her midriff in an unconsciously protective gesture.

'So,' she said, moistening her lips with a wary tongue, 'what more can I say?'

'You can tell me how my father's modest plans to build an extension to the original building turned into this place,' he replied, spreading his arms. 'When I left, he'd built the marina and was talking about putting in a swimming-pool and some tennis courts. Nothing like this.'

India lifted her head. 'Well—it seemed like a good investment, that's all.'

'To whom?'

'To—all of us,' she replied, choosing her words with care.

'But it must have cost the earth!'

'It was worth it.'

'Was it?' He came up the final step so that he was standing beside her. 'Your mother had big ideas, and my father would have done anything to please her.'

India stepped back. 'Your father was proud of what he'd achieved!'

'But it was a strain, right?'

'If you're implying that his heart attack had anything to do with money worries, you couldn't be more wrong!' she exclaimed angrily. 'My God! This place is worth a small fortune! Well, not small. Quite a large fortune, actually. How dare you suggest that his illness was in any way to do with the hotel?'

Nathan's face was unrelenting now. 'Well, you have to admit the old man did die years sooner than anyone could have expected,' he retorted, and India's stomach hollowed at the realisation that in a matter of minutes he had lost all veneer of politeness. He was cold and arrogant, and every bit as aggressive as her mother had expected.

'I don't have to listen to this,' she hissed, aware that the heat of their exchange was being monitored by at least two members of the staff. Paolo was obviously straining his ears to hear what was being said, and the young woman on the reception desk couldn't help noticing that something was wrong. 'If you have any complaints, I suggest you take them up with Mr Hastings when he gets here. I don't want you upsetting my mother any more than she's been upset already.'

Nathan scowled, but when he spoke it wasn't Adele he was interested in. 'Hastings?' he said. 'He's coming here?'

'In a couple of days, yes.' India found it much easier to cope with this conversation with the cloak of hostility between them. 'I asked him to delay his arrival, to give you time to familiarise yourself with the island again. Of course, I didn't know then that you were going to start throwing accusations around as soon as you got here.'

Nathan's jaw clamped. 'I'm not throwing accusations around. Hell, India, I'm just trying to find out what's been going on! Dammit, he was my father!'

'I know.' India squashed the feeling of sympathy that stirred inside her. 'But that doesn't give you the right to come here and impugn the reasons for his illness. You just might have played some part in that yourself!'

CHAPTER THREE

THE morning air was always cool, deliciously so, and one of Nathan's favourite occupations had been to take a stroll along the beach before anyone else was about. He saw no reason not to do so now, even if he hadn't slept in a bed. At this hour, the sand was clean and untrampled, without the prints of other feet to deny his isolation.

Nevertheless, he was well aware that his actions were not wholly innocent. By delaying his return to the hotel, he was deliberately putting off the moment when he would have to deal with the situation his father's will had created. Sooner or later, he would have to come to a decision about what he was going to do, but for the present he preferred to avoid a confrontation.

He had spent the night aboard the *Wayfarer*, more at home on the yacht on which his father had taught him to sail than in the absurdly opulent suite India and her mother had allotted him. In his more generous moments, he supposed it wasn't really their fault. What did you do with someone who was, yet wasn't, a member of the family? Particularly someone who was not welcome in the family apartments of the hotel.

Even so, he had guessed that Adele would be expecting to see him. How had she taken his father's death? He couldn't believe she was devastated by the tragedy. Only by what it had precipitated. The night before, he had actually anticipated the prospect of telling her to get out with some satisfaction. But that was before he had spoken to India, before he had discovered that she, and not Adele, had been running the hotel.

That was why he had taken himself off to the marina, guessing, accurately as it turned out, that no one would come looking for him there. He had needed time: time to consider the situation, time to think. He couldn't get rid of Adele without getting rid of India as well, and, in spite of what had happened, he found he didn't want to.

It was crazy. He knew that. Even thinking about keeping her on was going against every grain of intelligence he possessed. She had sided with her mother. She, like his father, had believed every word her mother had said. But, what the hell, she had only been thirteen! What kind of objectivity did a thirteen-year-old possess?

His father had left her future in his hands. That bugged him, too. Was the old man so sure he'd be magnanimous? Or didn't he care what happened to either of them—Adele or her daughter? Hell, what did he know about India, come to that? He'd been away for eight years. She might be more like her mother than he thought.

Beyond the marina, the coastline scalloped in a series of rocky coves. The sand here was pink-tinged, untouched, too rigorous for the lotus-eaters at the hotel to reach. They were the coves where he had spent his childhood, shared with no one until India had invaded his life.

He grimaced. How sentimental could you get? And he had believed he'd banished all sentimentality from his soul. Yet there was no denying that India did hold a special place in his heart. She was his stepsister, dammit. It wasn't something he needed to be ashamed of.

It was after eight when he got back to the hotel, and he was hungry. He'd made do with a sandwich the night before, but now he fancied eggs and bacon, and lashings of buttered toast. Not the kind of diet he recommended at a Sullivan's Spa, but exactly what he needed to fill his groaning stomach.

Breakfast was apparently served in the Terrace Restaurant, a sunlit octagon overlooking the ocean. It was a room made almost completely of glass screens, which could be shaded or rolled back, depending on the weather. At present, several of the screens were open, and a pleasant draught of air kept the temperature in the low seventies.

Nathan paused in the doorway, looking round the attractive room. Circular tables, each spread with a crisp white cloth, were set with gleaming silver and crystal glasses. There was the scent of warm bread and freshly brewed coffee, and his stomach rumbled in sympathy with the pleasant thought of food.

'Can I help you, sir?'

A white-coated waiter was viewing him rather doubtfully, and Nathan realised that, as on the previous day, his appearance wasn't winning him any friends. It was the first time he had considered that an overnight growth of beard was bristling his jawline, and that his shirt and trousers bore witness to the perils of salt water.

'I...' He hesitated, and then, deciding that however disreputable he appeared he was hungry and this was *his* hotel, he plunged on. 'Yes,' he said. 'Just point me to a table, and fetch me a pot of coffee, will you? I'll let you know what else I want after I've studied the menu.'

The waiter tucked the menu he was holding under his arm as he considered his response. 'Er—you are a guest of the hotel, are you, sir?' he enquired, his tone just bordering on unfriendly, and Nathan nodded.

'Room 204,' he agreed, deciding not to embarrass the man. 'Now—where do I sit? That table there—in the window?'

The waiter lifted one shoulder. 'I—I'm not sure,' he was beginning, when a familiar female voice intervened.

'I'll look after Mr Kittrick, Lloyd,' India declared smoothly, bringing a look of horror to the waiter's face. 'Oh—didn't Mr Kittrick introduce himself? Nathan, this is Lloyd Persall. He looks after our morning guests.' She gave him a considering look. 'He's particularly good if they have a hangover.'

Nathan felt a sense of resentment stir inside him. 'Good for Lloyd,' he intoned, in no mood to get into another argument with her. 'So what do I do to get some service around here? Produce my ID or what?'

India's lips tightened. 'Get Mr Kittrick what he wants, Lloyd,' she said, dismissing the discomfited waiter with a reassuring gesture. 'I'll take care of his seating arrangements.'

'Yes, Miss Kittrick.'

The waiter looked as if he wanted to say something more, but thought better of it, and Nathan waited, somewhat irritably, for India to indicate where she wanted him to sit. Damn, he thought, was this the kind of treatment guests came back for?

The table he was shown to was the one he had chosen in the window. A table for two, it was shielded from the glare by clever tilting of the vertical blinds, while yards of white tulle billowed in the breeze.

Despite his irritation, he felt obliged to say something after he was seated, and, offering India a faintly perfunctory twist of his lips, he said, 'Thanks. I guess I'll have to have my picture circulated to the other members of the staff if I want to avoid any more embarrassment.'

India stretched her arms to thigh level and linked her hands together. It was a vaguely protective gesture, though she seemed not to be aware of it. 'That won't be necessary if you allow me to introduce you to the rest of your employees,' she said, her tone clipped and reproving. 'If you hadn't disappeared yesterday evening, you'd probably be known by now. Our grape-vine is quite efficient, and you are creating quite a stir.'

Nathan lay back in his chair and looked up at her. Although he realised her remarks were justified, he knew a quite unwarranted desire to disturb her composure. Was this what happened when familiarity gave way to estrangement? Why did he want to treat her differently now, when she was obviously doing her best to keep it civil?

He refused to consider that the way she looked had anything to do with his attitude. The short pleated skirt and collarless white blouse were an unlikely incentive to his mood. The fact that they were black and white again respectively, as her outfit had been the day before, seemed to point to their being a kind of uniform, even if the cap sleeves did reveal her arms, and the skirt expose her legs from mid-thigh.

Even her hair had been confined in a French plait, and the tight way she had drawn it back from her face should have added severity to her profile. But it didn't. Instead, the austere style revealed the purity of her jawline, and the delicate curve of cheeks, which were as flawless as a peach.

God! The words flooding into his head appalled him. Appalled him, and disgusted him, too. He didn't want to analyse exactly what he was thinking, but when his gaze drifted from her face to the taut thrust of her breasts emotions of a different kind caused the harshness in his voice.

'I didn't "disappear" last night,' he corrected her shortly, suddenly aware of the tightness of his trousers. He shifted in his chair, trying to find a more comfortable position, and concentrated on the menu lying on the table in front of him. 'I just needed a little time to myself, that was all. I'm sorry if I inconvenienced you—and your mother—but I didn't know I had to inform you of my whereabouts.'

India's intake of breath was revealing. 'No one's saying that, Nathan——'

'Then what are you saying, then?' he demanded, slanting a gaze up at her vivid face. Yes, that was better, he thought; she was angry with him now. It was easier to deal with anger than combat her cool control.

'My mother expected you would want to see her,' she declared at last. 'That's not so unusual, is it? For heaven's sake, Nathan, she was your father's wife. Whatever grudges you may still bear her, she has taken Aaron's death badly. They'd been together for almost fourteen years! Can't you show a little consideration?'

Consideration? Nathan was tempted to ask what consideration Adele had ever showed towards him. But India wasn't to blame for her mother's duplicity. She was innocent of any treachery. Innocent of malice.

'Look, why don't you sit down and we'll talk about it?' he suggested, seeing Lloyd fast approaching with his coffee. 'Hey, that's great,' he added, as the waiter set a jug of freshly squeezed orange juice and a steaming pot of coffee on the table. He gave the man an approving smile. 'Just what I need.'

Lloyd looked relieved. 'Your eggs and bacon are on the way, sir,' he exclaimed. And then, after casting a doubtful glance in India's direction, 'I'm sorry if I caused you any upset earlier, Mr Kittrick. If I'd known——'

'No sweat.' Nathan could afford to be magnanimous. 'Miss—er—Miss Kittrick will be joining me for breakfast. Perhaps you'd like to take her order as well.'

India looked as if she wanted to refuse, but propriety won the day. 'Er—just toast and coffee, Lloyd,' she declared as he ushered her into her seat. And then, as the waiter went away again, she appended, 'Don't make my decisions for me, Nathan. I'm not a schoolgirl now.'

Nathan absorbed her anger as he poured himself a glass of golden juice. 'Will you join me?' he asked, gesturing towards her glass, but she turned it upside-down, and stared mutely out of the window.

With her profile turned towards him, and her determined chin supported by the knuckles of one hand, Nathan was able to watch her undetected. Despite the beauty of her complexion, she looked tired, he thought. Tired, and troubled, and he guessed Adele had given her a hard time when he had failed to show up the night before. Her knuckles shifted, and she brushed her hand across her cheek, revealing short, rounded nails, only palely tinged with polish. Her fingertips brushed the faint shadows beneath her eyes, and drew his attention to the slender arch of her brows. And when his eyes moved to her mouth, he knew his control was slipping again.

In consequence, he chose speech to arrest the madness, his tone less than conciliatory as he plunged into the fray. 'OK,' he said, after swallowing half the orange juice at a gulp, 'd'you want to tell me what's bugging you? I preferred to spend last night coping with my own grief, instead of trying to console someone who's never shown me any favours, and you're peeved. Is that it? Hell, India, I wouldn't even be here if Adele had had her way, and you know it.'

India removed her elbow from the table, and turned, somewhat reluctantly, he thought, to face him. But unlike him, she didn't immediately rush into speech. On the contrary, she seemed to consider her words with care before voicing them, her fingers plucking nervously at the linen napkin beside her plate.

'I think,' she said at last, 'that we—that is, my mother and I—would like to know what you intend to do with—with the hotel——'

'For hotel, read you and your mother,' interrupted Nathan cynically, as bitterness once again focused his mind. 'Adele wants to know if I'm going to have her thrown off the island, just as she once had me.'

India's eyes widened angrily. 'You can hardly compare the two instances. And as I recall it, it wasn't my mother who caused you to be thrown off the island, it was you! How can you even mention what happened then in the same breath as what's happened now? My God, I knew you'd changed, Nathan, but I didn't know how much!'

She would have left him then. She would have thrust back her chair and stormed away from the table, without giving him even half a chance to defend himself. She was flushed and indignant, resentful of any criticism he might make about her mother, her wide eyes accusing, her lips tightly compressed.

But she was not in control. When his hand shot out and fastened about her wrist, forcing her to stay at the table, he found she was trembling. Beneath the façade of angry defiance, she was shocked and uncertain, trying to cope with her own grief, but still vulnerable to his demands.

'Don't go,' he muttered, almost against his will, and meeting her defensive gaze with weary eyes. Lloyd was coming back with their breakfasts, and the last thing he wanted was their apparent animosity providing gossip in the staff quarters, he told himself grimly. The fact that India's wrist was slim and fragile, that her skin was as soft as silk, and that her bones moved sinuously beneath his hand meant nothing. Nor, when he moved his foot, and his deck shoe brushed against her ankle, was his reaction anything more than an automatic reflex.

He had to let go of her when the waiter reached the table, but his eyes held hers, compelling her to stay where she was. It wasn't easy, particularly when those wide-spaced blue eyes seemed to be staring into his soul, and he badly wanted to recoup his defences. But eventually her lids dropped, the tawny sweep of her lashes brushing her cheekbones, and he gathered himself sufficiently to greet the waiter without restraint.

'If there's anything else...'

Lloyd was understandably sensitive to the tension around his new employer's table, but Nathan managed to dismiss him with a contrived smile of approval. 'Nothing else, thanks,' he said, lifting the silver lids to expose creamy eggs and crisp curls of bacon. 'This looks great.'

If Lloyd had expected India to endorse her step-brother's statement, he was disappointed. Although she permitted him a brief glance, her lips remained tightly sealed, and Nathan realised his appetite had dissipated along with his mood.

Ruthlessly squashing the urge to put her mind at ease, he determinedly ladled a generous helping of the eggs and bacon on to his plate. There were rolls for him, too, and warm English muffins, wrapped in a basket, and he helped himself to a croissant and spread it thickly with butter.

It wasn't easy to eat with India sitting silently across from him, particularly when every mouthful was an effort to swallow. But he was damned if he was going to give Adele any food for satisfaction, and he knew his ruse was working when India's eyes drifted to his face.

'That's very bad for you, you know,' she said, as if the words were dragged from her, and Nathan's lips twisted at the automatic reproof.

'Don't you have anything positive to say?' he asked, round another mouthful of bacon. 'Like—"how have you been, Nathan? What have you been doing?" Or—"did you get married? Do you have a family?"'

India's eyes sought his. 'Do you?'

'Do I what?'

Her soft mouth tightened. 'Have a family,' she replied through clenched teeth.

'Not that I know of.' His response was deliberately casual.

'And a wife?' It seemed she had to ask. 'That is—are you . . . have you been married?'

Nathan hesitated. 'Married—no.'

India stared at him frustratedly for a moment, and then reached for the coffee-pot. Apparently she needed something to occupy herself as well, and he noticed, almost inconsequentially, that she still liked her coffee white.

'What about you?' he countered, although he could see there were no rings on her fingers. No betraying marks either. If she had been married or engaged, there was no evidence of it.

'No.' She used the coffee-cup as a kind of shield between them. 'Not yet,' she appended briefly, and he wondered somewhat jealously what that was supposed to mean.

He finished as much of the eggs and bacon as he could manage, and then pushed his plate aside. At least his physical self was satisfied, he thought wryly. But it was amazing how hollow he still felt inside.

India was staring down into her coffee-cup. As if it might give her the answers he was withholding, he mused without humour. What did she expect him to do now that he was in sole control? He might own Pelican Island, but it was still her home.

'My father,' he said at last, compelled at least to try to understand why the old man had made his will in his favour. 'If you were running the hotel, what did he do?'

India looked up, and then set her cup carefully on its saucer. 'He—spent a lot of time at the marina.'

'He didn't—travel—with your mother?'

'He seemed to prefer to stay on the island,' she admitted after a moment. 'He said it was because he was getting too old to go gallivanting off around the world.

I wonder now if he had already had some warning of his condition.'

Nathan's jaw hardened. 'Did he see a doctor regularly?'

'Only the local doctor.'

'Lennox?'

'Yes.'

'But Lennox was already past retiring age when I went away. My God, he must be seventy-five, if he's a day.'

'Seventy-six, actually,' said India levelly. 'But Daddy—Aaron—wouldn't see anyone else. He said he was OK. And, apart from some depression, he seemed to be so.'

'Depression?' Nathan focused on that word. 'What do you mean—depression? He wasn't suicidal or anything, was he?'

'No.' India was indignant. 'He was just—down sometimes. The doctor who examined him after—afterwards said it was a common symptom of heart disease.'

'Damn!' Nathan twisted his napkin into a knot and flung it on the table. 'Why the hell didn't he contact me? God, the man was dying, and he didn't even bother to let me know!'

'I expect he thought you wouldn't be interested,' remarked a high, cultivated voice, and Nathan lifted his head to find his stepmother standing arrogantly beside his table.

It was eight years since he had seen Adele, and the years hadn't entirely been kind. Oh, she was still a good-looking woman. Her streaked blonde hair looked as natural as the most expert hand could make it, and even at this hour of the morning her make-up was immaculate. But a free-flowing shirt over a plain black vest hid the bones and hollows that being too thin in middle age could expose. And she had not made the mistake of wearing tight-fitting trousers. Her loose-fitting Oxfords were made of silk, and billowed about her legs.

She was what? he wondered in those first few seconds, before contempt and common decency brought him to his feet. Forty-six? Forty-seven? He had never been absolutely sure of her age. When she had married his father, it had been something of a moot point, and she had always behaved as if she was more his contemporary than her husband's. Now, though, she was fighting a losing battle, and having a daughter who looked like India must make it very hard indeed.

He might have felt sorry for her even now if she had been able to put the past aside and treat him with respect. But the current of bitterness ran too deep, and her words were not intended to heal any open breach.

Predictably, it was India who replied first, hurrying into speech, as if anything she said could erase the cruelty of Adele's remark.

'Oh—Mother!' she exclaimed, pushing back her chair and getting up from the table, 'I didn't think you were awake yet. I looked in on you before I came over to the hotel, but you were fast asleep.'

'My eyes were closed, India, but I was not asleep,' retorted Adele shortly, as Nathan levered back his own chair, and came up beside them. 'I haven't slept a wink all night, as you should know.'

Nathan was sorely tempted to make use of that comment, but scoring points was not going to soothe his frustration, or bring his father back. And this woman had been his father's wife, his father's choice. There had to be a way to deal with this without losing his temper.

India was looking worried now, and he guessed she was afraid of what he might say—or do. For some strange reason, she still cared about the reputation of the hotel, and he knew he wouldn't do himself any favours if he let Adele call all the shots.

So now he forced back the urge to tell her what he thought of her greeting, and his voice was only gently mocking as he intoned, 'Still as tactful as ever, Adele. It's good to know you're glad to see me. I must admit, I never expected such a welcome.'

Adele's lips compressed. 'I suppose you think this is all very amusing, don't you? Playing games with people's lives. Making fun of our adversity. How Aaron could have done this to us, I really don't know. What did we ever do to deserve it?'

Nathan could have told her, and she knew it, but, like everything else, it was not something he cared to exhume. Besides, it was a relief to know that she still hated him. On that level, at least, they could meet on equal terms.

'Anyway, I didn't realise you had this little tête-à-tête planned for breakfast, India,' her mother continued coldly, as if not wholly trusting her stepson to reply without malice. 'Last evening you denied all knowledge of his whereabouts.'

'We didn't plan anything——' India was beginning tensely when Nathan chose to intervene.

'She didn't know where I was last night,' he declared, looping his thumbs into the belt that rested low on his hips. 'I'm sorry if you think it was thoughtless, but that's not my problem. I needed some time to think about what I'm going to do. And sleeping in that plush suite you've given me just didn't seem the place to do it.'

Adele's lips twisted. 'So you slept on the beach instead?' Her cold eyes swept over him. 'It's probably more what you're used to.'

Nathan absorbed the insult without comment. Then he ran a brooding hand over the stubble on his jawline. It was probably well deserved, he admitted ruefully. He should have used the bathroom before making this appearance.

But, 'No,' he said at last. 'No, sleeping on the beach is not my style, Adele. And, just for the record, I spent the evening at the marina. Ralph Davis still remembers me, and it was quite a relief to see a familiar face.'

'If Ralph let you sleep at the clubhouse...' began Adele sharply, and then, remembering Nathan's position, she pressed her lips together. 'Well,' she added, 'do I take it you're prepared to talk about the future now? Or must we wait for Arnold Hastings to turn the knife in the wound?'

Nathan heard India's sigh, and then she exclaimed, somewhat wearily, he thought, 'I don't think there's any point in being antagonistic, Mother. Whatever—whatever Nathan decides to do, we don't have much choice but to go along with it. And it'll be far easier all round if we try to be civil with one another.'

'Oh, yes?' Adele's thin brows arched, and she gave her daughter a scornful stare. 'Well, at least I know where your sympathies lie, India. Tell me, what do you hope to gain from this unseemly misalliance? What kickback has he offered you to turn against me?'

'Nothing!' India gasped, her indignation evident in the hot colour that invaded her cheeks. 'I know how you feel, Mother, and I do sympathise with your position. But fighting among ourselves isn't going to solve anything.'

Adele didn't bother to answer her. Instead she looked at her stepson, and Nathan met her brittle gaze with unexpected ambivalence. He guessed Adele was learning what it felt like to be helpless and frustrated, and he wondered what she was thinking as she faced her nemesis.

'You will give us enough time to make other arrangements, I hope,' she declared, scarlet-tipped nails plucking at the handful of gold chains she wore about her throat.

'What little money Aaron left us will not go very far towards providing the kind of accommodation we're used to, and I should like a few days to mourn my husband in peace.'

Nathan absorbed her words silently. Contrary to the way he had felt when he had first learned that his father had left him the island, he discovered he could pity Adele. He didn't forgive her for what she had done to him. That was still too painful to ignore. But time did have its compensations, after all.

'No one's saying you have to leave, Adele,' he essayed at last, and in the pregnant silence that followed his words he had plenty of time to wonder at his reasons for saying them. But it was too late now. The die was cast. And although Adele still looked suspicious, there was a trace of relief in her expression.

'What—what is that supposed to mean?' she asked eventually, when it became apparent that her stepson was not about to elaborate. 'Do you mean we can stay?'

'I'm saying that no one's forcing you to give up your home here,' he replied evenly. His eyes flickered to India's anxious face, and the faint sense of well-being he had felt at his own generosity faltered. 'Whatever—whatever my father's reasons were for leaving me in charge of the hotel, I can't believe he would want me to ignore my responsibilities.'

Adele's tongue circled her upper lip, drawing his attention to the faint beading of sweat that had appeared there. Evidently she had expected an entirely different response, and, not for the first time, he wondered if there was more to his father's decision than a simple desire to redress the balance.

'Well,' she said at last, and there was no mistaking the relief now, 'I must say I didn't expect you to be so reasonable, Nathan. Obviously age and——' her eyes flicked over his lean, muscular body, arousing emotions of a much less hospitable kind '—experience have given you a maturity beyond your years.' Her gaze moved consideringly to her daughter, and there was speculation as well as triumph in her eyes. 'Of course, India will welcome your decision, even though she was most insistent that you would want us to leave. She's had me in a state of panic ever since the will was read.'

CHAPTER FOUR

INDIA wished her mother hadn't said that.

Standing at the open doors leading on to the gallery outside her room, watching the setting sun painting the exotic colours of the garden with its golden radiance, India wished her mother wouldn't always shift the blame for any misconceptions on to her. She had never said anything to cause Adele the slightest anxiety. She wouldn't do it. And it was frustrating to be accused in front of Nathan.

Not that it was the first time such a thing had happened. When her stepfather was alive, her mother had often used her as a scapegoat when Aaron found her out in some lie. Oh, they were small things mostly: she hadn't delivered a message Adele had given her, or her mother had been with her, when India had known full well she hadn't. Adele had always made the excuse that Aaron was too possessive, that he wanted to know where she was every minute of the day, and that she needed some privacy. She said it was only fair that India should support her. After all, she'd add, they were blood relations, and if it hadn't been for her India might have been living in some filthy squat in London.

And India had never let her down. Much as she had loved Aaron, she would never have betrayed her mother to him. Adele had given up a lot to ensure that she had a *real* home, a *real* family. If it hadn't been for her, Adele could have resumed her modelling career after her own father had died.

Of course, Adele had fallen in love with Nathan's father, even though he was so much older than she was, and it hadn't really been such a great sacrifice to leave their small, congested apartment in London and move to the Bahamas. But India had never been allowed to forget that, without the responsibility for her small daughter, Adele might never have considered marrying again. Particularly someone who had proved so lacking in ambition.

Even so, what had happened this morning had disturbed her. There had been no need for Adele to pretend she had been agitating for them to leave. Heavens, last night her mother had been sure Nathan was about to 'boot them out', as she'd put it. How could she accuse India, when it was she who had tried to reassure her mother?

India sighed now, and tipped her head back against the cool column of the door-frame. She had thought, now that her stepfather was dead, that she and Adele might grow closer together. They hadn't been close in recent years, but that was mainly because India had been so tied up with the hotel and her mother had spent a great deal of time visiting friends in the United States. They had never had the kind of relationship common among the young people and their parents who visited the hotel. Theirs had always been that one space removed from a real rapport.

But even now, it seemed, they were as far from sharing their lives as ever. Adele didn't want a friend, she wanted a co-conspirator, and India felt a certain amount of resentment at being made to tell lies to Nathan, of all people.

Not that she'd seen Nathan for the rest of the day. She knew—because her secretary had told her so—that he had spent most of his time in his father's office, going over the previous years' accounts. He had asked for the codes of current expenses, profit and loss, and projected estimates for the coming months. Using the computer hadn't fazed him at all, and, whatever he had been doing these last few years, he was not unconversant with current business practice. It was obvious he wanted to learn as much as he could about the company's assets before Arnold Hastings arrived on the scene, and India could only speculate on his motives. She wondered if it meant he was thinking of selling the hotel in the not too distant future. Whatever promises he had made to her mother, she was not convinced he would put their interests before his own.

And did she truly want to continue supervising the hotel if Nathan planned to stay on the island? She might pretend she hardly knew him, that he was a virtual stranger to her, but the fact remained that he was not. The events of that evening when her stepfather had thrown him out were not forgotten, only put aside. And although she had determined not to think about it, she was already getting goose-bumps at the memory of that night.

Besides, there would always be the echoes of the childish infatuation she had felt for him between them. Somehow, because Nathan had gone away, perhaps, those feelings had never been satisfactorily erased. It wasn't that she still cared about him—not in that way, at least—but she still felt a kind of nostalgia for the innocence she had lost.

More immediately, there was the fact that he had undermined her authority. Like when he had reprimanded Paolo in the bar. And appearing at breakfast unwashed and unshaven, as if he was deliberately flouting their conventions to prove how little he cared. Even his method of retaining her company at the breakfast-table had shown her how arrogant he was. Her wrist had ached for hours after he had grabbed it. Though, when she'd examined it later, she hadn't been able to find any bruises.

Probably it was just her extra-sensitivity where he was concerned, she admitted wearily. Since their heated exchange the night before, she had been waiting for him to make some response. Yet, even when her mother had given him every opportunity to endorse her opinion that India had behaved badly, he had chosen not to comment. Possibly he was waiting for a better occasion to show his hand, she reflected. A clever adversary never played all his cards at once. He always tried to keep something up his sleeve.

Maybe she wouldn't be feeling so strung out if she'd slept the previous night, she thought tiredly. But seeing Nathan again, having that set-to with him, had left her more unsettled than ever. She'd wanted to handle his arrival so calmly, to prove to him that she was no longer the impressionable teenager she'd been when he'd gone away. But somehow it had all got away from her, and now she had the feeling that she was running out of rope.

She tried to remember how she'd felt when she'd first learned that Nathan might be coming back to the island. There'd been some alarm, some regret, even some bitterness, until logic—and her own common sense—had recognised that Nathan could have had nothing to do with his father's decision. Maybe the lingering grief she had felt for his father had been responsible for the reluctant sense of anticipation she had felt as she'd driven to meet him at the airport. But when he'd climbed down from the plane she'd realised that the dream and the reality were something else.

He had changed so much. Not only in appearance—although he was taller and much more physical than she remembered. For a moment, she had scarcely recognised the boy who'd gone away in the tough-looking man who had answered her greeting. But for all his cool-eyed cynicism, her response had been the same, and it was this, as much as anything, that plagued her now.

The trouble was, he apparently still thought he could treat her like a child. He had proved that, driving in from the airport. Had she changed so little since that night eight years ago? Or was she just too vulnerable to any kind of criticism?

She wished now she had taken Steve with her. He had wanted to go along. He had realised—obviously better than she had done—that she might not find the situation so easy to control. And he had been right. And, if Steve had come along, Nathan would have had no chance to tease her, or leave her feeling that she was still a child as far as he was concerned.

But perhaps she was over-reacting yet again. Certainly, later in the evening he had been left in no doubt as to her feelings of resentment. She just wished she hadn't let him upset her. But his remarks about his father had been totally unforgivable.

Of course, her response had been fairly nasty, too. But the truth was that Nathan's accusations had touched an unwilling chord inside her. Although Aaron had seemed enthusiastic when they had first devised the blueprint to make Kittrick's one of the great hotels of the world, there was no denying he had had misgivings later.

The trouble was, at barely fourteen, India had been too young to have an opinion that mattered. She'd had no conception of what her mother's suggestion might involve. She had only seen the dream, not its composition. And the enormous liability it entailed had obviously fallen on her stepfather's shoulders.

She sighed. Had she been selfish? Had her mother been selfish? For her part, she had welcomed the idea as a way to relieve the sense of betrayal she had felt over Nathan's actions, and she had been more than willing to accept Adele's assertion that Aaron felt the same. It was what he needed, her mother had declared. Something new and exciting to help him put the past firmly behind him. But it didn't look now as if it had succeeded. Or why else had he brought Nathan back into their lives?

Yet Aaron had taken his son's deception badly. In spite of his love for his second wife, and his genuine affection for India, Nathan had held pride of place in his heart. A circumstance Adele had resented, until subsequent events had changed things.

Even now, India couldn't think of what had happened without reliving her own sense of betrayal. She was far beyond the point of wondering how he could have done what he did, but the fact remained that the mystery had never been satisfactorily resolved.

She had always believed he had loved his father just as much as Aaron had loved him. He might have resented his father's marrying again. It was true that he had always treated Adele with respect, but there had never been the easy relationship between them that there had between Nathan and herself. Or that was what she, in her innocence, had thought. With hindsight, she had decided it was his attraction towards his stepmother that had caused him to act as he had. An attraction that had become irresistible, and which he had come to believe her mother had returned.

Why he had believed such a thing, she couldn't imagine. She was not blind to her mother's failings, but she couldn't believe Adele would have encouraged his advances, a fact that had been proved the morning her mother had flown screaming from his bed; that awful morning when Aaron had disowned his son forever.

Though not forever, as it had turned out, India admitted now. And no one, least of all her mother, had anticipated what Aaron had done. To make Nathan his heir! To give his son everything that Adele—and India—

had worked so hard to create had been nothing short of criminal in her mother's eyes. The fact that Adele had never made any actual financial contribution to the scheme was unimportant, she maintained. She had given Aaron everything, and he had left them penniless.

Well, not quite penniless, India conceded, remembering the huge insurance policy Aaron had taken out, making her mother the sole beneficiary. But, compared to the value of Pelican Island, she supposed it was fairly negligible. And, without Nathan's generosity, they would have found it hard to start again.

So why was Nathan being so generous? she wondered, unwillingly aware of the more obvious explanations. Did he still feel some attraction for her mother, even after all these years? And what was Adele likely to do about it, if it proved to be the case?

India shivered. There was something distasteful in even considering such an alternative. Yet it was true that before Adele had appeared that morning he had deliberately avoided talking about the future. She had asked him what he was going to do, and he had neatly evaded an answer. But when her mother arrived at the table he had been swift to reassure her.

What had happened after her mother made that frivolous remark about her behaviour, India didn't know. Rather than stay there and listen to any more lies, she had excused herself and left them. And, in all honesty, she had spent the rest of the day avoiding them both. She didn't care what happened, she told herself. She was beginning to think they deserved each other.

India put up a hand, and lifted the weight of her hair away from her neck. The garden was darkening as the quickening twilight cast long shadows between the palms. The breeze that caused the tops of the trees to sway was cool against her heated flesh, but inside she could feel a solid core that felt as cold as ice.

Was it really only a little over two weeks ago that Adele had attended the reading of the will, looking pale and poignant in her black lace dress? Naturally, that had been before she'd known the contents of the will, before Mr Hastings had exploded his bombshell.

Of course, her mother had been shattered by Mr Hastings's announcement. The image of the demure, grieving widow had swiftly given way to one of incredulity and bitterness. She had left the office with tight lips and angry protestations, swearing she would fight the will that she was sure was false.

But, of course, it wasn't false. Arnold had assured them of that. And, when she was calmer, he had warned her mother against doing anything that might jeopardise any chance of dealing with Nathan in an amicable fashion. His advice had been to stay and wait for further developments.

Which still didn't explain why Aaron should have taken the course he had. Had he been so unhappy? What motive had driven him to reach out to his estranged son?

The phone started to ring in the room behind her, and, almost grateful for the diversion, India went to answer it. Any minute now she would have to get ready for the dinner with Senator Markham and his wife that she had postponed from the night before. But any delay was welcome. She was in no hurry to see Nathan again.

Of course, it could be Nathan on the phone, she reflected as she picked up the receiver. But it was too late now to pretend she wasn't in. 'Er—India Kittrick,' she stated, hearing the brittle tone in her voice. And then a feeling of relief flooded her as a familiar male voice answered, 'No kidding? And I thought you'd left the island!'

'Steve!' She said his name on a heavy sigh. 'You're back!'

'Hey, I've been back since two o'clock this afternoon,' Steve Whitney responded drily. 'Where the hell have you been, Dee? I've been trying to reach you for hours.'

India took a moment to regain her composure. The fear that it might indeed be Nathan had dug deeper than she'd thought. Though why she should be so reluctant to speak to her stepbrother she couldn't imagine. Except that she kept remembering his reaction to her mother.

'I've been—busy,' she murmured now, realising it wasn't much of a reply, but in no mood to discuss her feelings with Steve. Not yet, at least. 'I—how was the trip? Did you do any serious fishing? I was going to come down to the marina, but I haven't had the time.'

She crossed her fingers as she said this. In all honesty, she'd had more time today than she'd known what to do with. But she and Steve had been friends since he'd joined the staff at the marina eighteen months ago. And, although their emotional relationship was still in its earliest stages, she was afraid he knew her well enough to know when something was wrong.

'We caught a couple of marlin,' Steve replied now, briefly describing the overnight charter he had handled. Since Aaron's death he had taken over many of her stepfather's clients, and although he wasn't the senior skipper he was experienced and efficient, and popular around the hotel. Indeed, the female guests in particular found his blond good looks and easy charm very appealing, and there were always two or three women hanging about the chandlery when Steve was in charge of the store. 'How about you?' he added, a note of concern entering his voice. 'I hear your prodigal brother's caused quite a stir.'

My *stepbrother*!

The correction trembled on the tip of her tongue, but she swallowed it back. The reason why she should feel the need to define their relationship so precisely was something she preferred not to think about. Besides, Steve knew perfectly well that Nathan wasn't related to her, not by blood, anyway. And, in any case, what did it matter? It wasn't of any significance.

'What have you heard?' she asked after a moment, avoiding a direct answer. 'He's only been here twenty-four hours!'

Steve hesitated. 'I heard he spent the night at the marina. Seems like the rooms you had picked out for him in the hotel weren't good enough.'

India sighed. 'I don't think that's entirely true. Oh, I'm not denying he spent the night down at the marina, but that was probably due to the strength of Ralph's specials. I seem to remember you sleeping at the clubhouse on occasion.'

'He didn't sleep in the clubhouse,' retorted Steve crisply, evidently not appreciating being reminded of his own shortcomings. 'He slept on your father's yacht. Horace found the cabin unlocked when he went aboard this morning.'

India frowned. Not that it mattered that Nathan had slept on the *Wayfarer*, but he might have said. The boat hadn't been touched, except for cleaning, since Aaron had died.

'It looks like you won't be leaving the island, anyway,' Steve continued more cheerfully. 'Is it true? Have he and your mother made their peace?'

'It—seems that way,' India admitted reluctantly. 'At any rate, we've got a breathing-space.' And that was as far as she wanted to go, she added silently. The reasons for and against staying here were no longer so clear-cut.

'So what are you doing for dinner?' he asked, and she was grateful for the change of subject. 'I've got me a juicy lobster, and I was thinking of baking it in a little lemon juice and butter. And I've got just the wine to serve with it: cool, of course, and just dry enough to sharpen your taste-buds.'

India felt a smile tugging at her lips. For the first time that day, she actually felt a glow of optimism. What did it matter what Nathan thought, or did, or believed about her? If her mother was foolish enough to believe everything he said, then that was her decision. She wasn't Adele's keeper, so why should she feel responsible?

'That sounds perfect,' she began, and then she remembered Senator Markham. 'Damn!'

'What is it?' Steve was wary.

'I can't,' she exclaimed disappointedly. 'I can't have dinner with you. I've got another appointment.'

Steve's voice tightened. 'What is it? A family affair?'

'No.' India was impatient. 'I've promised to eat with Senator Markham and his wife. He wants to discuss holding a pre-caucus conference here in December. It's just going to be a small affair for party helpers and their wives. But he wants to get it organised before he flies home tomorrow.'

'So why don't you ask your brother to deal with it?' suggested Steve tersely. 'I mean, it was OK working every hour God sent when you thought you were going to own the hotel one day. But the old man's shown you what he thinks of your efforts, and let's not pretend that, while no one's throwing you out, the situation hasn't changed.'

India chewed on her lip. 'I—can't do that, Steve.'

'You mean you won't.'

'I promised the senator——'

'And what did your father promise you, hmm? Or don't you want to think about that either?'

India moistened her lips. 'We could meet after dinner.'

'Yeah. We could.' Steve sounded angry now. 'But I might just have another appointment, right? See you.' And he rang off.

India was putting the finishing touches to her make-up when her mother appeared at her bedroom door. 'I did knock,' she said defensively at her daughter's indignantly raised eyebrows, indicating the door into the sitting-room behind her. 'But you obviously didn't hear me.'

'Obviously.' India struggled not to sound as irritated as she felt. It wasn't her mother's fault that Steve had shown so little understanding of her position, and she surveyed Adele's appearance with determined objectivity. 'You look nice.'

'*Nice*!' Her mother made the word sound almost like an insult. She smoothed her hands over the thick amber-coloured satin that cleverly disguised the slenderness of her hips. 'Darling, is that the best you can do? I thought I looked quite stunning.'

'Well, you do, of course.' India put down the mascara brush she had been using, and turned away from the dressing-table. 'I gather you're feeling better. Will you be joining the Markhams and me for dinner?'

'Heavens, no.' Steve would have approved of Adele's response. 'As a matter of fact, I'm eating with Nathan. He wants to talk about his plans for the hotel before Arnold arrives in the morning.'

The sharp pain of resentment that shot through India at these words was no less agonising because it was unexpected. So that was why Adele had taken such pains with her appearance, when for the past couple of weeks she had hardly cared what she looked like. Of course, the image of the grieving widow had suffered a severe set-back when they had first learned of Nathan's involvement, but this was the first sign that her mother's devastation was not as deep-seated as India had believed.

'Is—is that wise?' she ventured now, turning back to the mirror so she didn't have to meet her mother's eyes.

'I mean, after what happened before Daddy threw Nathan out. What will people think...?'

'Things were different then,' retorted Adele shortly. 'I was a married woman, for one thing.'

'You were his father's wife,' India reminded her tautly. 'And now you're his father's widow. What's the difference?'

'The difference is that we've all got older, wiser...'

'But don't you think your sudden—conversion might raise a few eyebrows?'

'D'you think I care what a few small-minded old biddies might think?' Adele touched her hair, which had been newly tinted, and was now as soft and pale as thistledown. 'And don't you look at me like that, India. Just remember, if it weren't for me you'd be looking forward to spending the rest of your life struggling to make a living!'

'Millions do it,' India muttered under her breath, but her mother heard her.

'Not someone who's lived in luxury for the past fifteen years,' she retorted swiftly. 'You won't get anywhere with that kind of attitude, believe me. I'll do whatever I have to to make sure we have a decent life, India. And if that means swallowing my pride and acknowledging Nathan as our benefactor, then what have I got to lose?'

India pressed her lips together. She didn't really know why she was arguing. After all, when she'd gone to meet Nathan the previous afternoon she'd been quite prepared to meet him halfway. The trouble was that from the moment he'd stepped down from the plane things had changed. She'd tried to tell herself it was just the changes in him—and in herself—that were responsible for the uneasy feelings she had, but something told her it was more than that. Deep inside, she'd known he meant trouble, and nothing that had happened since had altered that conviction.

But, 'All right,' she said now, viewing her own appearance with a deepening sense of gloom. Beside Adele's delicate colouring, she felt brash and garish. Even the simple black sheath she was wearing did little to tone down the colour of her hair, and after this exchange with her mother there were matching flags of colour in her cheeks. 'Have a nice evening.'

'I shall.' Adele turned, and a cloud of Dior perfume drifted to India's nostrils. 'You, too,' she added, pausing in the doorway. 'I'll tell Nathan you're looking after his interests, shall I? I'm sure he'll be impressed.'

'No, I...'

India started to tell her not to talk about her at all, but Adele was gone. The slamming of the outer door was proof that this had just been a courtesy call; her mother's only reason for coming here had been to forewarn her of what to expect.

CHAPTER FIVE

NATHAN helped himself to more wine, and then lay back in his seat, ostensibly listening to the music that drifted out on to the terrace. In passing, he had to admit that India was right. Carlos was a damn good pianist. But more immediately his attention was fixed on the occupants of a table at the other side of the dining area.

The good-looking senator, who was fifty if he was a day, was setting out to charm his youthful companion. Nathan had heard of Woodrow Markham, had seen his picture in the tabloids from time to time. He was usually photographed with a beautiful woman. Film stars, models, society hostesses, they all seemed to fall for his rather boyish appeal. He had quite a reputation with the ladies, and it was no secret that his wife of some twenty-five years was used to looking the other way when some attractive female caught her husband's eye.

And India was certainly attractive, thought Nathan grimly, watching her response to some quip the good senator had made. Hell, she was a beautiful woman, mature, and probably experienced, and clearly capable of holding her own with someone as obvious as Woodrow Markham. So why did he feel like charging across the terrace and attacking the older man with his bare hands? Why did his fingers itch to haul the man up out of his seat, and his fist ache to bury itself in his smug, smirking mouth? It wasn't because he felt sorry for the rather tired-looking woman who sat on his right and fidgeted constantly with the stem of her wine glass. And it wasn't because the man had ever done him any harm. Dammit, it was men like Senator Markham who had helped make him a millionaire.

India laughed suddenly, and the delightful sound caused several heads to turn in her direction. She actually seemed to be having a good time, thought Nathan broodingly. Like mother, like daughter! Why had he expected anything else?

'India seems to be enjoying herself,' remarked Adele lightly, and Nathan forced his attention away from the object of his displeasure. Damn, he'd asked his stepmother to have dinner with him in the hope of discovering more about the reasons why his father had changed his will in his favour, but since India had walked on to the candlelit terrace he had found it impossible to concentrate on anything else.

'Er—oh, yeah,' he acknowledged shortly, as if his stepsister's appearance had gone unnoticed. 'Markham has that effect on women.'

Adele's lips curved in a faintly malicious smile. 'Some women,' she amended, abandoning the spiced venison on her plate in favour of her wine. 'I find Woodrow's *bonhomie* just a little bit over the top.'

'It seems to work, though,' Nathan persisted, not really knowing why, but reluctant to change the topic. 'Do you know him well? Is he one of your regular guests?'

Adele shrugged her thin shoulders. She was wearing a gold sequinned jacket over a sleek satin sheath, but it couldn't quite hide the narrow bones that moved beneath her skin. 'He's been here a couple of times,' she conceded offhandedly, raising her glass to her lips. 'Many of the state governors have been here from time to time. We attract all the best people, Nathan. Even the Vice-President has paid us a visit.'

Nathan's mouth compressed. 'How nice.'

'Yes, it was, actually.' Adele met his lazy gaze with some indignation. 'Both the Vice-President and his wife are charming people. Why, I even had a drink with them one evening. They complimented me on our success.'

Nathan's dark eyes narrowed. 'Friends in high places.' His tone was mocking. 'You set your sights high these days, Adele.'

'I do what I have to do,' she retorted, and then, as if aware she had spoken a little too vehemently, she forced a tight smile. 'I can't help it if people enjoy my company, Nathan.'

'Why would you want to?' He swallowed a mouthful of the fine claret he had ordered to accompany the venison, and returned her smile. 'But I think we're at cross purposes, Mama. I was talking about men.'

Adele's lips tightened. 'I'm not your mama, and I don't appreciate your humour, Nathan. And if you're implying that my relationship with the Vice-President was anything other than discreet——'

'How about Markham?'

Adele stared at him coldly. 'I think you must have taken leave of your senses, Nathan. Just because you once misunderstood the—the affection I showed towards you, don't judge everyone by your own standards!'

'I didn't misunderstand anything,' retorted Nathan harshly. 'And you know it. So don't let's have any distortions between us. We both know what really happened, and it's better if we forget it.'

Adele's face was frozen. 'If you'll excuse me...'

'I won't.' As Adele picked up her purse, and moved as if to get up from the table, Nathan's words arrested her. 'I won't excuse you, and I won't forgive you, but I am prepared to tolerate your staying here for India's sake. And——' he looked at her over the rim of his wine glass '—if you want to remain on the island, I suggest you stop deluding yourself and start accepting the status quo.'

Adele's nostrils flared. 'How dare you speak to me like that?' she hissed. 'If your father had known half of what you said to me, he—he'd have killed you!'

'Would he?' Nathan tilted his head. 'If I'd told him how you used to come to my room, wearing only the flimsiest of nightwear, he might have killed you instead.'

Adele's lips twisted. 'He'd never have believed you.' She laid her purse beside her place again, and then, taking advantage of Nathan's silent acknowledgement, she added, 'Besides, you were wrong. You over-reacted. How was I to know you'd be aroused by my appearance? I was your stepmother, darling. I only wanted you to love me.'

'Love?' Nathan said the word scornfully. 'As in have sex with you, you mean,' he countered in an undertone. 'Poor Adele, always so desperate for affection! What did you hope to achieve, I wonder, getting into my bed like that?'

'Shut up!' Adele leant towards him angrily, and Nathan guessed she was itching to slap him now. 'You wanted me, Nathan,' she appended, her fists clenched between her breasts. 'I touched you, remember? I felt your reaction. A man's body isn't like a woman's. It gives him away every time!'

Nathan's lips curled. 'You really think my arousal was anything to do with you?' he taunted. 'Hey, that's what happens every morning, with or without your participation!'

Adele drew back in her chair. 'You're disgusting!'

'And you're frustrated,' remarked Nathan flatly. 'Grow up, Adele. You can only fool *all* the people *some* of the time.'

The music ended with a flourish, and in the lull between pieces their plates were cleared. 'Would you like to see the dessert menu, Mrs Kittrick?' asked their waiter, hard on the heels of the busboy, and, although he addressed Adele, he included Nathan in his request.

'Just—coffee. Thank you,' Adele answered, after a moment, and Nathan nodded briefly, endorsing her reply.

But, in all honesty, he would have preferred a long cold beer. It was a warm evening, and even the huge fans that were meant to cool the terrace were only circulating the warm air. He was just considering the advisability of unbuttoning his collar and loosening the knot of the tie he had bought in the swish men's boutique that afternoon, when his attention was caught by the man who had stopped at Senator Markham's table. Tall, broad-shouldered and blond, with the kind of husky physique that made the senator look rather scrawny, he was evidently well known to all of them. India was looking particularly animated, and under cover of the table, and out of Markham's view, she squeezed the young man's hand with evident approval.

Unwilling to draw attention to his interest, but incapable of denying the question, Nathan nodded across the terrace. 'Who's that?'

Adele, who was apparently still brooding over his last words to her, shifted irritably. 'Who?'

Nathan contained his impatience. 'At the senator's table,' he said evenly. 'D'you know him?'

Adele cast a disgruntled look over her shoulder, and then her lips curved into a knowing smile. 'Oh—you mean Steve,' she said, and Nathan knew that somehow she had sensed his dissatisfaction. 'Steve Whitney,' she expanded, clicking her fingers for the wine waiter to come and refill her glass. 'Haven't you met him yet?'

'Obviously not.' Nathan forestalled the waiter, and filled her glass himself. 'What does he do? Pump iron? Give massages? What?'

'He does look like that, doesn't he?' Adele permitted herself another smug glance in his direction. 'And I have to say, I don't think India uses him to his full potential. But your father hired him to skipper one of the charter vessels, and in his spare time he works down at the clubhouse.'

Ignoring the innuendo, Nathan frowned. 'I didn't see him there last night.'

'No, you wouldn't.' Adele sipped her wine. 'He took out an all night charter late yesterday afternoon.'

Nathan nodded, but he didn't make any comment. He was too busy watching what was going on at the senator's table. To his intense annoyance, the senator appeared to have invited Whitney to join them. He was sitting down now, next to India, and her face was alight with welcome.

Nathan was aware that Adele was still watching him, and that giving her this kind of ammunition wasn't perhaps the most sensible thing he had done in his life, but he couldn't help it. His eyes felt as if they were glued to the little tableau being enacted at Senator Markham's table, and it wasn't until the waiter brought their coffee that he compelled himself to look away.

'They do,' Adele remarked silkily, after the waiter had set out the cups, coffee-pot and cream jug, and departed, and Nathan gazed at her blankly. 'Sleep together,' she expanded, taking evident pleasure in the admission. 'Our little girl has grown up quite a lot since you went away, Nathan. She knows all about what happens to a man's body in the mornings.'

His jaw hardened, but he managed not to show his anger. 'Does she?' he countered lightly, realising that any kind of reaction on his part would precipitate a response. 'No sweat!'

Adele stared at him disparagingly. 'Don't pretend you're not interested. I've watched you looking at her.

Seeing her with Steve really bugs you, doesn't it? What's the matter, Nathan? Are you jealous?'

'Just—curious,' he replied, irritated with himself for allowing his feelings to get the better of him. 'I guess now that my father's dead I feel some responsibility for her.'

'Like hell!' Adele's mouth was ugly. 'Who do you think you're kidding, Nathan? D'you think I didn't notice what was going on before you left here? God, the kid was besotted with you! Why d'you think I split you two up? Because I was afraid you might take advantage of her.'

Nathan's whole being recoiled. 'You're sick, Adele,' he told her violently. 'India was what—thirteen or fourteen when I went away? Far too young to understand anything about sex!'

'You weren't,' remarked Adele blandly, and he could tell by her expression that she knew she had struck a nerve. He had been aware of India's girlish hero-worship before he left the island. And it had been hard sometimes, when she'd fought with him, or teased him, or beat him at chess or tennis, to remember she was seven years younger than he was. She had always been tall, and, being around adults all her life, she had seemed older than her years. She had been his friend and his companion, and, though he'd sensed her warm affection, he'd known it for what it was.

'It's a pity she doesn't know what a bitch she's got for a mother,' he observed harshly. 'Perhaps I should tell her.'

'She'd never believe you,' replied Adele calmly, and, although it galled him, he knew she was right. God, if he hadn't been able to convince his own father, how in hell could he hope to convince someone who had so much more to lose?

The pianist started to play again, and Nathan made a valiant effort to recover his equanimity. Dammit, he thought, did it really matter what Adele said, or what India thought? He had had the last laugh, hadn't he? Whether his father had ever had doubts was something he would probably never know. But the fact remained that the old man had left Pelican Island to him. To run—or close down, he realised, with a rare spurt of malice.

'Anyway,' Adele continued at last, and he was relieved when she didn't refer to India again, 'have you decided what you're going to do?'

Nathan took a deep breath. 'About what?'

'About the hotel, of course.' There was a more cautious note in Adele's voice now. 'I don't suppose you know anything about what it takes to run a hotel of this size. If you want my advice, you'll leave it to India, and the professionals she employs.'

'I employ,' corrected Nathan evenly, unable to resist the small amendment. 'As to what I intend to do, I haven't made any decisions yet.'

Adele frowned. 'But you do intend to keep it open!'

'Perhaps.'

'What do you mean, perhaps?'

'Just that.' Nathan shrugged his broad shoulders. 'I haven't made up my mind. It's not the way I remembered it, I'll give you that. In the old days,' he added, deliberately baiting her, 'I didn't have to wear a tie to come in to dinner. And, if I wanted to go fishing, I didn't have to book a craft.'

Adele caught her breath. 'Have you any idea how popular this place is? Why, this one resort is more successful than half a dozen other resorts put together. People queue up to get bookings here. In high season we're booked years in advance. Your father was a millionaire, Nathan. And he didn't get that way by catering for sailors who cared as little for how they looked as what they ate!'

'No.' Nathan's mouth compressed. 'No, you changed all that, didn't you, Adele? Dad's dream of a little island paradise catering for people like himself soon went out the window. As you said, he didn't get to be a millionaire by doing what he wanted. And what I have to ask myself is, did he want to be a millionaire?'

India and her boyfriend were on their feet, bidding goodnight to Senator Markham and his wife, when Nathan reached their table. Although Adele had retired to the cocktail bar some time ago, he had remained on the terrace, emptying the second bottle of wine he had had the waiter bring him after his stepmother had left. He wasn't drunk, exactly, although he wasn't used to such serious drinking. But he was rather pleasantly anaesthetised, and only peripherally mindful of the intrusion his appearance represented.

'Senator; Mrs Markham,' he greeted them politely, before turning his attention to the others. 'India,' he acknowledged. 'I wonder if we might have a few words. I'd like to clear a few things up before Hastings arrives in the morning.'

India was obviously embarrassed, and in some distant, lucid corner of Nathan's mind he knew he was responsible. But the warmth and reassurance of the wine provided a secure barrier between his words and his conscience, and he met her gaze innocently, half amused by her nervous reaction.

'Er—do you know my stepbrother, Senator?' she asked, as the man sitting beside her turned to give Nathan an uncertain look. In his shoes, Nathan thought he would have regarded himself with less tolerance. But perhaps Whitney thought his salary was more important than India's self-respect.

'I don't believe I do,' Woodrow Markham was saying now, putting his napkin aside and getting to his feet. 'Pleased to meet you, Mr Kittrick. Damn fine hotel your family's got here.'

My 'family' is dead, Nathan thought broodingly, but he had no real grievance with Markham, and it would be foolish to promote one. So, 'Thank you,' he responded, aware that India was watching him with anxious eyes.

'Won't you join us for a drink, Mr Kittrick?' suggested the senator, ever the politician. 'Your sister and young Whitney here were just about to take a stroll on the beach. I'm sure whatever it is you have to talk to her about can wait till tomorrow, can't it?'

'I'm afraid not.' Nathan knew he was being boorish, but he couldn't help it. He looked at India again, seeing the hostility in her eyes, but indifferent to its message. 'You'll excuse us, won't you—Whitney, is it? This is *family* business. I'm sure you understand.'

India's expression warned him that she wouldn't understand if he went through with this, but the wine was making him indifferent to her pleas. Besides, he was damned if he was going to sit here making small talk with Markham while Whitney took her for a romantic stroll along the beach.

Steve Whitney lifted his broad shoulders in a dismissive gesture. 'Well,' he said, 'if it's important——'

'It is,' Nathan assured him, and, just to be sure India knew he meant it, he slipped his fingers around her arm just above the elbow. She was holding her arms clamped to her sides, and in consequence the backs of his knuckles brushed the warm, yielding swell of her breast. But he had hardly had time to register the reaction that it had on his recalcitrant body before it was withdrawn. With an abrupt movement, she severed any contact, and put Steve Whitney's bulk between them.

'Looks like you're not being given a choice, India, girl,' Markham averred ruefully. 'But business is business, as I know to my cost; isn't that right, Loretta?'

Anyone who looked less like a Loretta, Nathan couldn't have imagined. Mrs Markham was small and nervous, with sandy-coloured hair, and washed-out blue eyes. It was as if all the colour had been washed out of her, Nathan reflected wryly. Was that what happened when you were married to someone as colourful as Woodrow Markham?

'That's right, Woodie,' Mrs Markham answered now, and while the senator was looking a little miffed at the diminution of his name she went on, 'We were very sorry to hear about your father, Mr Kittrick. He was a good man. A gentleman, as we say where I come from. He'll be sadly missed.'

'Well—thank you,' Nathan was murmuring, rather taken aback himself now, when Senator Markham hurried in with his own tribute.

'Loretta and I've had several delightful breaks here in the past few years,' he concluded. 'Your father and your stepmama, they looked after us real well.' He winked at India. 'Not forgetting your little sister, of course.'

Nathan managed not to look as cynical as he felt. Until Mrs Markham had mentioned his father's death, the genial senator hadn't even given it a thought. He felt sorry for Loretta. Married to someone else, she might have made something of herself. As it was, she was forever in his shadow, forced to play second fiddle to a man who treated her without respect.

'I'll say goodnight again, then,' India inserted now, giving Steve Whitney a rueful smile, even as her eyes flashed daggers at Nathan. 'If I don't see you before, I hope you have a pleasant journey home. And I'll pencil in your request, Senator. Perhaps your secretary will get back to me as soon as you have a definite date.'

'That she will, that she will.' The senator held on to India's hand several seconds longer than was necessary before transferring his grip to Nathan. 'Hope to see you again on my next visit, Mr Kittrick. Maybe you and I could do some business together. I've got a piece of land in Arizona, just right for one of your developments.'

Nathan blinked. Until that moment, he'd assumed the senator knew as little about his business interests as India and her mother, but he had been wrong. Markham evidently made it his business to know everything about the people he was dealing with, and when it had been announced in the Press that Nathan was the new owner of Pelican Island certain enquiries must have been made about his background.

Aware that India was only half attending to what was being said, Nathan's response was necessarily brief. He wasn't ready yet to tell India—or Adele—about his company. It was simpler for now to let them think he was still feeling his way.

'I may get back to you on that, Senator,' he agreed, stepping round Whitney, and taking a firmer hold of India's elbow. 'Now—if you'll all excuse us...'

India made her feelings felt as soon as they were out of earshot. 'How dare you?' she demanded. 'How dare you barge in on a private party and drag me away like some latter-day Neanderthal? If you'd wanted to talk to me, you should have done so during office hours.'

'I tried,' replied Nathan evenly, resisting her attempts to break free of him without much effort, and enjoying her subsequent frustration. 'You didn't come in to your office once today, and your secretary couldn't—or wouldn't—tell me where you were.'

India sucked in her breath. 'I've been busy,' she retorted. 'And I didn't realise I had to keep you informed of my whereabouts. I've been—about the hotel, if you'd cared to look for me. I've done what I'm supposed to do, and I'm not going to be cross-examined at half-past ten at night about something that's really none of your business!'

'Isn't it?' As Nathan guided her down the steps away from the pool deck, and into the scented cloister of the garden, he gave her a questioning look. 'Forgive me, but, if you wish to continue drawing a salary from the hotel, won't I be expected to pay it?'

India's eyes registered the kind of hurt mortification he would never have wished to promote. 'If you don't approve of the way I do my job, you can always fire me,' she declared, through lips that were being manfully controlled. 'There's nothing we have to discuss that couldn't have waited until tomorrow morning, and you know it. I don't know why you're doing this. What have I done to deserve it?'

Nothing—except show up for dinner looking like any man's fantasy, thought Nathan broodingly. The black sheath she was wearing clung to every curve of her glorious figure, and the precarious knot she had made of her hair was just begging to be tumbled. As it was, several tendrils of fiery silk curled invitingly beside her ears, and the nape of her neck was proudly arched and vulnerable in the moonlight.

'I wanted to talk to you,' he said now, allowing her to break free of him once they'd reached the beach. He watched as she wrenched off first one high-heeled sandal, then the other, and realised she was wearing no stockings when her toes sank into the damp sand.

Not that she needed them, he reflected. Her long legs were smooth and textured like cream. There was a slit in her skirt that revealed her calf and a glimpse of one knee as she moved, and he thought how ironic it was that that fleeting exposure should possess more sensuality than a miniskirt. Nevertheless, he could imagine how her skin would feel beneath the clinging fabric, imagine sliding his hands above her knees to the soft warm flesh between her thighs...

'What about?'

Her question momentarily fazed him, and he cursed himself anew for allowing his thoughts to take the turn they had. My God, was Adele right? Had he entertained such thoughts about India all those years ago?

But no. No matter what her mother said, what ugly doubts she tried to plant in his mind, nothing would persuade him he had ever thought of India as anything more than his little sister. And, if he'd never gone away, perhaps that was how he'd still see her. But he had gone away, and things had changed. She wasn't his faithful shadow any more, and for some crazy reason he resented it.

'How long have you known Whitney?'

It wasn't what he had intended to ask. He had been struggling to put his mind back on track, and the question had come out of nowhere. But it was obviously of more importance to his subconscious mind than what he had learned from the profit and loss accounts that morning. And, in any case, there was no way he could retract it.

'Does paying my salary entitle you to ask personal questions as well?' she enquired coldly, and he had to admit she had a point. It was nothing to do with him how long she had been involved with Steve Whitney, and she had every right to refuse to answer.

But something—some inner demon perhaps—drove him on. 'Humour me,' he urged, giving in to the relief of loosening his collar and his tie. 'Pretend I'm your guardian. I mean, now that my father's dead, I suppose I do stand *in loco parentis*.'

'Like hell!' Her reaction was vehement. 'I'd rather have a snake for a guardian than you!' She planted her feet in the sand and turned to face him. 'And just for the record, don't imagine that because you can twist my mother round your little finger you can do the same to me!'

Well, that was clear enough, he thought grimly, trying not to show how angry her bitter remarks had made him. Although if she had heard their conversation this evening he doubted she would have felt the same. Nevertheless, 'Adele has her own reasons for trying to mend bridges,' he told her shortly. 'You seem to forget, she's the only other person, besides myself, who knows what really happened that morning. She also knows I have the power to blow her little boat right out of the water. Why wouldn't she be friendly? She's got a lot to lose!'

'You mean you're blackmailing her into accepting you,' retorted India recklessly, and he realised suddenly how desperately she wanted to believe that. Just for a moment, he had a glimpse of the real India, the frightened, confused child she had been when he had gone away. She wanted to believe her mother, but his presence was disturbing her. Not half as much as she was disturbing him, he admitted briefly, before her tear-bright eyes seduced his reason.

'God, India,' he groaned, his hands moving of their own accord to bracket her bare shoulders, sliding sensually against the soft flesh. 'What kind of a monster do you think I am?'

Her eyes sought his, then dipped away, but not before he had seen the uncertainty in their depths. She wanted to discredit him just as much as she wanted to keep faith with her mother. It would make it easier—but the ties between them were still powerful enough to give her pause.

And then it all became irrelevant anyway. What she was hoping; what she was thinking. It didn't matter. The night; the moonlight; the perfume that drifted from the dusky hollow between her breasts and enveloped him in its spicy fragrance; the awareness of their isolation, and her vulnerability; it was all too much. Too much for him; too much for his inflamed senses.

Afterwards he blamed the wine. He had drunk too much. And eaten too little. That was true as well. But, at that moment, the whys and wherefores were of no account. Only his desires mattered, and they were painfully apparent. He was holding her, touching her, but it wasn't enough. He wanted her. He wanted to feel that slim, luscious body pressed against his. He wanted her to feel his hardness, to know what she was doing to him. But, first of all, he wanted to feel her mouth beneath his, and the moist heat of his tongue between her lips.

Sanity spun beyond his control. His hands on her shoulders tightened, strengthened. He was drawing her towards him firmly, but inexorably, and although she came unwillingly he knew she had no idea what he intended. Perhaps she thought he wanted to comfort her. He had comforted her in the past, when bruised elbows and scraped knees were all he had had to worry about. Perhaps she thought he was making amends for the embarrassment he'd caused her earlier. Although her eyes were dark in the shadows, they glinted with unshed tears, and in a lucid corner of his mind he guessed she wanted to believe in him.

But it was too late for him to have second thoughts. Too late to care about his memories of the past. India wasn't a child any longer; she was a woman. Her breasts were firm where they nudged his chest, her long legs incredibly sensuous against his thighs. And, when his hands slid from her shoulders, down the bared column of her spine that was exposed by the halter neckline of her dress, and settled on the swell of her hips, it was all he could do not to cup her bottom and bring her more intimately against him.

As it was, he was sure she must be able to feel the hardness straining at the zip of his silk trousers. Trousers he had bought that afternoon, at the same boutique as his tie. They were expensive, and cool, but regrettably thin, and there was no way on earth he could disguise his arousal.

But what the hell, he thought recklessly as his hands spread across the delicious curve of her hips. It wasn't as if he was in any doubt about what he wanted. God, her hips were so smooth, and he didn't believe she was wearing any underwear. His breath quickened uncontrollably, and his touch became a caress.

'Nathan!'

Her breathy use of his name was both a protest and a question, and, as if sensing what was happening here was no simple apology, her hands came up to brace his chest. Beneath her hands, his heart thudded wildly, and he wondered how two nervous palms could burn right through his shirt.

'India,' he said, his voice breaking on the word, and, avoiding her opposition without effort, he bent his head and brushed his lips against her cheek.

She shivered—there was no other word for it—but she wasn't cold. Her breath, escaping her lungs in jerky gulps, was hot and humid, and when his fingers touched the hollow of her spine, where her dress formed a provocative V, the skin was damp and pulsing with heat.

'Let me go, Nathan.'

She got the words out with an evident effort, but he paid them no mind. For all her resistance, she was trembling, and it was easy to convince himself that she didn't mean what she said. Besides, the scent and warmth of her body was drowning any lingering hesitation, and when his hands shaped her rounded rear and lifted her fully against him there was no turning back.

God, she felt so good, her legs separating to accommodate his sex, her hands skittering from his chest to his neck and back again. She might have wanted to go on resisting him, but her own body was betraying her, and when his lips sought hers she turned her head—but not quickly enough.

Her mouth was like hot silk, and, although his first kiss barely grazed the corner, his hand at the back of her head soon corrected that omission. With a hunger he hadn't known he possessed, he ground his mouth against hers, and the cry she uttered was stifled by the urgent invasion of his tongue.

He felt the sudden flare of awareness that leapt inside her. In spite of herself, her hands clutched him then, gripping the overlong hair that lapped his collar, and hanging on as if her life depended on it. Her mouth opened to his like a flower, and when his tongue came again she suckled on it greedily.

Dear God! His senses swam, and a haze of pure, unadulterated lust swept over him. He could feel her breasts against his chest, round and full, their shape palpably evident through the fine material of her bodice. He could imagine how they would look with that frail barrier torn away, how her whole body would look, naked in the moonlight. His heart quickened. He could hardly breathe. His lungs felt as if they were being squeezed, and yet he sought her mouth again and again, unable to get enough of her sweetness.

And she was responding. Her lips were soft now, pliant, endlessly receptive. Her fingers stroked his neck, seeking, caressing, sending a shaft of hot desire down into his abdomen. It settled low, between his thighs, and the ache became unbearable.

'Oh, baby,' he groaned, feeling a masochistic delight in prolonging his torment, and she moved against his swollen flesh as if she knew exactly how he was feeling.

She was all female, all woman, and his choked 'I want you' was as much a paean to her beauty as an admission of his own physical need.

But when his fingers reached for the knot at her nape that kept the halter in place her hand was there before him. 'No,' she said unsteadily. And then, when his eyes darkened with a mixture of disbelief and impatience, 'Not—here.' She glanced uncertainly about her. 'Someone—someone might see.'

Nathan blinked, struggling to assimilate what she was saying through the deafening roar of his blood. Not now, his senses were screaming. She couldn't be stopping him now. What did he care if they were seen? He wouldn't live with the pain of her rejection.

But she wasn't rejecting him, he realised swiftly. And, in a small corner of his mind, the core of what she was saying made sense. The beach was quite deserted, but it was tolerable at best. He had the sudden notion to see India in his bed, naked between his sheets...

'Let me go back first,' she breathed now, tucking away the strands of her glorious hair that he had dislodged. She took a breath. 'My room opens on to the terrace at the back of the annexe. Do you know where that is?'

Nathan moistened his lips. 'I have a general idea.'

'Good. Well—my window is the first. I'll leave it ajar. Give me five minutes and follow me.'

Nathan hesitated. 'Isn't my room——?' he began, but she interrupted him.

'In the hotel?' she chided. 'I don't think so. The annexe is much more private. And you can easily reach the terrace from the garden.'

'OK.'

Her acquiescence was flattering, and Nathan had no choice but to agree. If he thought there was anything suspicious about her willingness to concede, he was still sufficiently high to make excuses. She had wanted him just as much as he wanted her. He just hoped the time it took to reach her room would not prove his undoing.

CHAPTER SIX

THE room was stuffy when India woke up. Hot and stuffy, she acknowledged uncomfortably. The shutters were closed and locked, the curtains drawn, and she had turned off the air-conditioning before she had got into bed. That was why the room was so airless, and why she had the beginnings of a headache.

Peeling the damp sheet from her legs, she sat up and thrust weary hands through her tangled hair. What time was it? she wondered, blinking sleepily at the clock. The discovery that it was half-past eight only added to her irritation.

She had overslept—and no wonder, she thought impatiently, paddling across to the windows, and dragging back the curtains. The sunlight glinting through the shutters only added to the ache in her temples, but she opened the windows and released the catch, and let the cooler air stream into her room.

Tipping her head back on her shoulders, she breathed deeply, feeling the immediate release of tension. But the tension in her body was a simple thing to cure; it was the tension in her heart that didn't falter.

Dear God, she fretted, what must Nathan have thought last night when he'd found she wasn't in the room she'd promised? How must he have felt when he'd stepped through those French doors and found the room empty? Her pulse raced at the thought of meeting him again, of confronting his angry accusations. But it was his own fault for misjudging her, for believing she'd let him seduce her.

Of course, that was why she'd locked and barred her own windows, and turned off the air-conditioning. She'd wanted nothing to indicate that any of the rooms were occupied—except the one she'd chosen, of course—and she'd lain there, tense and anxious, until exhaustion had got the better of her.

She shook her head. Her mother was right. He was totally without conscience. He had prevented her from going off with Steve, and completely ruined her evening. As well as treating her like some cheap tart who'd fallen into his arms without hesitation.

Oh, he'd been drinking. She knew that. And, in the circumstances—and perhaps with someone else—she might have been prepared to overlook his behaviour. But Nathan was Nathan. He knew exactly what he was doing. And, after all that had gone before, he'd still had the gall to abuse her.

Abuse?

She felt a momentary flicker of guilt ripple through her body. That was a strong word, and she wasn't totally comfortable with using it. Nathan hadn't *abused* her, exactly. But he had taken unfair advantage. He had used his power as her stepbrother to make her do what he wanted, and had then conveniently forgotten their relationship when his libido had come into play.

She shivered. The trouble was that, if she hadn't exactly encouraged him, she had done little to discourage him. She had uttered the odd word of protest here and there, but from the moment Nathan's mouth had sought hers she had been putty in his hands. It was only sex, she knew that. She might be inexperienced, but she'd known what he was doing when he'd thrust his tongue into her mouth. And he'd been so hard, the throbbing shaft of his manhood taut and disturbing against her stomach. There had been an uncontrollable high in knowing that she could do that to him.

And maybe he'd have succeeded in his objective, too, if he hadn't said he wanted her. It was those words—and their terrible association with her mother—that had cooled her blood, and brought her swiftly to her senses.

India had been fourteen when 'it' had happened, but she still remembered that morning as if it were yesterday. It was her mother's screaming that had wakened her, that had sent her stumbling from her bed in her nightshirt into the upper corridor of the old house. She hadn't known what was happening, of course. Not then. She had been alarmed, but not frightened, imagining, foolishly, that Adele must have found a spider in the shower. Adele had always been afraid of spiders, and it wasn't the first time she had run shrieking from the bathroom.

But she soon realised her mistake. Even as she had opened her door, her stepfather had gone charging past her, with a sobbing Adele at his heels, and she had hurried after them, more curious than anything else.

She remembered that Nathan's door had been open before they had got to it, and she'd followed her mother and Aaron inside in wide-eyed confusion. If she'd thought anything at all in those brief, anxious moments, it was that something must have happened to Nathan, and her first reaction had been one of relief at finding him alive and apparently in good health. He was still in bed, lying against his pillows, with only a sheet to cover his obvious nakedness.

Not that that had surprised her. She'd known he slept nude, ever since one morning when she'd entered his room unannounced and surprised him getting out of bed. He'd roared at her then, and she'd quickly retreated, but not before her startled gaze had registered the sleek, muscled power of his anatomy. It had been her first initiation into the differences between the male and female form, and for weeks afterwards she had filled her drawing pad with sketches of Nathan in a variety of nude poses. Of course, she had destroyed them all before she'd gone back to school. She would have hated for him—or anyone—to see them.

But Nathan hadn't roared at her that morning. It was Aaron who had been shouting, accusing his son of trying to seduce his stepmother. As she'd stood there, frozen with horror, she had understood why her mother was crying. Nathan had tried to make love to her, and Adele had fought him off and run screaming from the room.

She remembered Nathan's silence as being almost deafening. He had just lain there, sombre and unblinking, allowing his father's tirade to engulf him. He'd said nothing, done nothing, made no attempt whatsoever to deny his guilt. And that was when Adele had sobbed that it wasn't her fault that he 'wanted her'.

India recalled little after that until she had been back in her own room. She seemed to remember backing away towards the door, and her action causing Nathan's gaze to turn upon her. But there had been such an expression of pain in his face that she doubted he had even seen her. He'd probably been too shocked, she thought bitterly. He must never have dreamed that her mother would betray him. As it was, he'd waited until later to tell his version of the incident to his father.

Which had only damned him further, she admitted wryly. It was obvious he'd needed time to come up with a convincing explanation. But to accuse her mother of trying to seduce him… India shuddered now, and walked grimly into her bathroom. Had he really believed that any of them would swallow that? Least of all herself. For heaven's sake, Adele was her mother!

The shower she took refreshed her, but she swallowed a couple of aspirin with a glass of water before leaving her room. She was under no illusions that today was going to be one of the most harrowing days of her life.

She just hoped Mr Hastings would arrive early. His presence was the only thing that might save her from Nathan's wrath.

Her mother was in the small morning-room that overlooked their own private patio. The patio was filled with pots and containers, spilling their colourful blossoms over the tiles, and echoed with the sound of the fountain that rippled invitingly into a sunken basin. She was sitting at the table, smoking a cigarette, crumbling the remains of a muffin between her fingers. She was staring out at the courtyard, evidently lost in thought, and India guessed she was not expected to join her.

'Good morning, Mother.'

Her greeting brought Adele's head round with a start, and she immediately stubbed out the half-smoked cigarette with nervous fingers. Then, as if realising how guilty it made her look, she deliberately reached for another cigarette from her bag.

'You see how you've got me,' she exclaimed. 'I'm a bag of nerves. What are you doing here at this time of the morning, anyway? Aren't you supposed to be in your office, planning menus or something?'

India sighed. 'I don't plan menus, Mother, and you know it.' She hesitated for a moment, and then pulled out a chair, and seated herself opposite. 'And if you want to kill yourself with cigarettes, that's your prerogative. If you remember, it was Daddy who used to complain about your smoking, not me.'

'You agreed with him.' Adele sniffed. 'And you still haven't told me what you're doing here.'

'I live here.' India gave her mother a wry look. 'But I slept in. Not that it matters.'

'But of course it matters.' Her mother looked at the unlit tip of her cigarette, and then pushed it back into the packet. 'You don't want Nathan to think you're dispensable, do you?'

India chose her words with caution. 'I'd say he already thinks that,' she replied evenly. 'Haven't you noticed? We don't exactly get along.'

Adele fidgeted with the knife beside her plate. 'He—said that?'

'Not in so many words.' India was reluctant to elaborate, but Adele was bound to hear about what happened anyway, and she wanted to get it over with. 'I—don't enjoy being made to look a fool in front of my friends.'

Adele glanced at her. 'How did he do that?'

'Last night.' India managed to sound casual. 'After you'd left the restaurant he came over to Senator Markham's table.'

Adele's eyes narrowed. 'He did?'

'Yes.'

'And?' Adele gazed at her encouragingly. 'Go on. What did he say?'

'It wasn't so much what he said.' India felt a beading of sweat on her upper lip, and hoped her mother would put it down to the undoubted humidity in the room. 'It was—what he did.'

Adele frowned. 'He didn't upset the Markhams, did he? If he's done anything to jeopardise——'

'He hasn't.' India broke into her mother's tirade to offer a weary denial. 'As a matter of fact, he and Senator Markham seemed to get along extremely well.'

She frowned suddenly, as the reminder of something the senator had said stirred a memory inside her. It was something about land—in Arizona. Yes, that was it. The senator had intimated that Nathan might be interested in the land for some development. But what did it mean? Had Nathan already decided to open another resort just like Pelican Island, but in the desert? If so, it must mean he had known about his father's will before he had died.

'India!'

Her mother's voice interrupted her reverie, and she realised she had been staring into space for several minutes. Adele's expression was a reflection of her impatience, and, gathering her thoughts, India tried to remember what she had been saying.

'Why?' Adele was asking now, and India looked at her in some confusion. 'Why did you say that Nathan and Senator Markham seemed to get along?' She licked her lips. 'You don't think they know one another, do you?'

'You mean before I introduced them?'

'Well, of course.' Adele was irritated now, and India wondered if she'd missed something while she had been speculating on their relationship.

But, 'No,' she assured her mother now. 'I don't think so. It was just—something the senator said.'

'What?' Adele gazed at her unblinkingly. 'India, are you trying to annoy me? For goodness' sake, spit it out!'

India shrugged. 'Well, it was nothing really. Just something about some land the senator owns in Arizona. He suggested Nathan might want to buy it.'

Adele pushed her plate aside, and reached for her cigarettes again. 'Land?' she echoed blankly, picking up the monogrammed book of matches that rested on the ashtray. She struck a match and lit her cigarette with a hand that wasn't quite as steady as it should be. 'Why would Nathan be interested in a parcel of land in Arizona?'

'I don't know.' India shook her head. 'As I said, it was just something the senator said, and Nathan made some comment about maybe taking him up on it. That was all.'

Adele's brows drew together. 'And what do you think it means?'

India gasped. 'Me? Hey, I don't have an opinion, Mother. I'm just telling you what was said.'

'So how did that embarrass you?' her mother exclaimed shortly. 'As far as I can see——'

'It didn't.' India stifled a groan. For a moment she had forgotten how this conversation had started, but now she was forced to retrench. 'He—embarrassed me by insisting he needed to talk to me, when it was obvious to everyone that he'd had too much to drink.'

'I see.' Adele paused. 'Well, I hope you didn't embarrass the Markhams, India. It cuts both ways, you know.'

India's indignation was cut short by the arrival of Josie O'Neil, who had taken care of the annexe and its occupants ever since it had been built. A sturdy black woman in her forties, Josie acted as both housekeeper and cook, and, although her duties were not arduous, she took them fairly seriously. She had also proved a good friend to India, and when she was younger she had often gone to Josie for comfort, rather than her mother.

'Well, now,' she said, regarding India's presence at the table with much the same surprise as Adele had shown earlier, 'don't tell me you haven't eaten.'

'I haven't. But don't worry.' India forced a rueful smile. 'I'm not hungry, honestly. I was just—keeping my mother company.'

'Nonsense.' Josie cleared Adele's dirty dishes on to the tray she was carrying, and wiped away the crumbs with a napkin. 'You can't work on an empty stomach. I'll rustle you up some eggs and a couple of pancakes. I'll be back with some fresh coffee in a jiffy.'

'No.' India stopped her before she disappeared out of the door again. 'That is—it's very kind of you, Josie, but——'

'Kind, nothing. It's my job.' Josie gave her a reproving look. 'Like I said to Mr Kittrick, if I didn't take good care of you, you'd be skinny as a rail. And heaven knows, since your Daddy died you haven't eaten enough to keep body and soul together.'

India sucked in her breath, and then glanced anxiously at her mother, half afraid she'd notice and be suspicious of it. But happily Adele seemed as intent on what Josie was saying as she was, and, with some misgivings, she ventured, 'You spoke to Mr Kittrick about me? This would be—Mr Aaron?'

'Heck, no.' Josie shook her head, shifting the weight of the tray to her hip. 'I'm talking about Nathan, India. Him and me had quite a conversation last night.'

'Last night?'

India said the words, aghast, but before she could say anything more to incriminate herself Adele intervened. 'Did you say something about fresh coffee, Josie?' she enquired pointedly, drawing heavily on her cigarette. 'And make enough for two, will you? Mine's gone cold.'

'All right, I'm going.' Josie pulled a face, but she seemed to take the hint. However, before she left, she couldn't resist one final retort. 'Can't see why he couldn't have stayed over here anyway,' she remarked. 'Seeing as how you and him had spent the evening together.'

The black woman departed with a defiant backward glance, but her words lingered in the air long after she had closed the door. They were sufficiently ambiguous for India not to feel they were noticeably directed at her, but that didn't prevent her from feeling guilty, or from giving her mother a swift, nervous glance.

'That woman is getting impossible!'

Adele's outburst was as unexpected as Josie's, but India was grateful for small mercies. 'She is?'

'Yes.' Adele stubbed out her half-smoked cigarette, and immediately reached for another one. 'I don't see that it's any business of hers what we do.'

India lifted her shoulders. 'I... imagine... she was just—making conversation,' she said awkwardly. She hesitated, and then, deciding she had nothing to lose, she added, 'I wonder what—what Nathan was doing here last night.'

Adele expelled her breath on a sigh. 'Oh—well—you might as well hear it from me as someone else; he came to see me.'

India's jaw dropped. 'What?' she whispered in a strangled voice, her mind buzzing with the inconsistencies of what she had heard. It couldn't be true.

'I know it sounds suspicious,' exclaimed Adele swiftly. 'And I have to say, I didn't invite him. But—well, he came to apologise.'

India stared at her. 'You mean—he came to your room?'

Adele had the grace to look a little embarrassed herself now. 'Yes.' She shrugged. 'He must have been in the garden and noticed that my window was open. I have to tell you, I got quite a shock when he stepped through the curtains. I didn't even know he knew where my room was.'

India felt sick. She had had no idea that Adele might leave her windows open. It certainly wasn't recommended, and most people used the air-conditioning to keep their rooms cool.

'So—what happened?' she asked faintly, trying to behave as if she was as shocked as Adele had been. Which she was, she thought grimly. Only not for the reasons her mother imagined.

'Well——' Adele seemed to gain confidence from her reaction '—I think he's still attracted to me. No.' This as India would have made some response. 'I know you'll think I'm crazy, but I'm inclined to forgive him.'

'*Mother*!'

'I mean it.' Adele was looking thoughtful now. 'After all, he's paid his penalty, hasn't he? For eight years he's had to scrub around looking for one job and another, trying to make a decent living, when he could have been living here in the lap of luxury. And why? Because he was foolish enough to fall in love with me!'

India shook her head. 'You don't mean that.'

'I do.' Adele lay back in her chair, and toyed with the handful of gold chains at her neck. 'I mean, let's face it; he is persistent, isn't he? And—I'm only human.'

India swallowed the bile in her throat. 'What happened last night, Mother? What did he do to make you think he—he's still in love with you?'

'Oh—nothing much.' Adele's eyes took on a reminiscent glaze. 'But you have to admit, it was romantic, coming to my room like that. I was quite—overwhelmed.'

India's fists clenched. 'Were you in bed?'

'Thankfully not.' Adele uttered a rueful little laugh. 'I shouldn't have liked him to see me unprepared and smothered in cream. No, I'd just arrived myself. He must have followed me from the bar.'

India pushed her chair back, and got up from the table. 'I—I've got to go,' she said abruptly.

Adele blinked. 'But you haven't had your coffee.'

'I'll get some later.' India groped desperately for an excuse. 'I—er—I promised Nicki I'd help her check the receipts. I've just remembered. And I want to get them out of the way before Mr Hastings arrives.'

'Well, if you're sure.' Adele regarded her consideringly for a moment, and then said, 'You wouldn't be upset about me and Nathan, would you, darling?'

'No!' India's denial was fierce, but she couldn't prevent that revealing colour from staining her cheeks. 'I—I just think you're mad, that's all,' she retorted bitterly. 'My God, Aaron's only been dead for two weeks. How can you even consider his replacement?'

CHAPTER SEVEN

NATHAN flung himself into the worn and cracked leather chair behind his father's desk, and ran tense, restless fingers over the arms. He remembered climbing into this chair when he was little, dragging it up to the desk and pretending he was in charge of the hotel. Only, of course, it had been a much more modest establishment in those days, and the desk this chair had faced had not been a giant slab of granite. He guessed his father must have held out when it had come to replacing his chair. It was the only thing in the office that reminded Nathan of him—that and the stern, unsmiling portrait on the wall.

He shook his head as he twisted the chair to look up at the painting. Having his portrait painted was not the sort of thing his father would have chosen at all. No doubt it had been done at his wife's bidding. It was just the sort of image Adele would want to promote.

Adele...

He groaned. God, he didn't know which of them had been the more astounded when he'd walked into her room the night before. He knew his face had frozen with horror, and it was just as well she had been too intent on stifling her own reaction to notice.

But the window had been open, just as India had said, and he had stepped into the room like a rat into a trap. The effects of the wine had been fading, but his blood had been just as hot. Too hot, he thought savagely, or he wouldn't have fallen so easily for India's deceit.

Nevertheless, it had cooled rapidly enough in the tense atmosphere of Adele's bedroom. She must have just arrived herself, thank God, because she had still been fully dressed. He didn't know what he'd have done if she'd already been in bed, with the lights out. Hell, his skin feathered with revulsion. He could just imagine what she would have made of that. And this time he wouldn't have had a leg to stand on.

His jaw compressed. But luckily it hadn't happened, no thanks to India. She had set him up, and the raw fury he had felt at her betrayal could hardly be contained. What was she trying to do to him? he wondered. Hang him twice over? Or was this her way of showing him what she thought of his excuses?

The ironic thing was that his initial reaction when he had seen Adele had been one of panic. Blind panic! God, he'd had some bad moments over the years: mornings when he'd awakened still shaking from his dreams; nights when he'd paced the floor, because closing his eyes only brought back the image of his father's accusing face. Dreams, *nightmares*, whatever he cared to call them, they'd all been the same—a subconscious replay of that God-awful morning when he'd opened his eyes and found his stepmother naked in his bed.

And, crazy as it seemed, that was how he had felt last night. It was as if his worst fears had been realised, and that he was twenty-two again, staring into Adele's seductive face. It didn't matter that eight years ago he'd thrust her tormenting hands away and pushed her out of his bed. He'd still been accused—and found guilty—of attempted rape.

Thankfully, last night the feeling hadn't lasted. If anything had been disposed to banish the last remnants of alcohol from his brain, finding himself in Adele's bedroom was it. Besides, he wasn't that naïve boy any more. He no longer assumed that just because he was telling the truth he'd be believed. He was a man now, with a man's thoughts and feelings—thoughts and feelings that had been toughened by the sultry heat of Central America. Where once his panic would have paralysed him, now it merely energised his brain. With the adrenalin pumping, he could handle any situation, control any emotion. Except... His lips twisted. Except when he was dealing with his stepsister...

Pushing that thought aside, he reached for the print-out lying on the desk in front of him. He had pulled the figures it contained earlier that morning, unlocking the office and using the computer long before anyone else in the hotel was out of bed. After what India had done to him the night before, he had been in no mood to sleep, and it had seemed as good a time as any to try to quantify his findings.

He sighed, threading weary fingers through his thick dark hair. In spite of the hotel's success and reputation, its financial position was decidedly poor. Hell, it was pathetic. It barely broke even on a day-to-day basis, and its long-term projection put it squarely into the red. And it was too simple to think that somewhere someone was siphoning off the profits. The underlying shortfall was too considerable for that. In his opinion, the hotel was too big and too expensive to run for the limited number of guests it could accommodate. Without a comprehensive change of approach, they were going to be in serious trouble.

What it needed was a huge injection of capital—but not to maintain the status quo. Either some of its facilities had to be phased out, or a building programme instituted to provide further accommodation. By his reckoning, they needed at least thirty more rooms in the short term to maintain its present high standards, with a corresponding increase in staff to ensure its five-star rating.

Quite a turn-around, he thought broodingly, throwing the print-out aside, and chewing on his lower lip. And from what he'd learned of India, he guessed she'd probably fight the proposition tooth and nail. She'd maintain that they'd lose their exclusivity, and perhaps they would. But, one way or another, the hotel had to start earning its way.

So why hadn't his father realised it? he wondered. Or had he? And without the necessary capital to expand, had he buried his head in the sand and hoped the problem would go away? But his accountants must have laid it out for him. On its present course, Kittrick's Hotel simply wasn't going to make it.

Which put a whole new light on his inheritance, he reflected grimly. Was that why the old man had left the hotel to him, and not to India and her mother? Had it become so much of a millstone around his neck that he hadn't wanted to unload it on to their shoulders? Most likely, he thought bitterly. Aaron Kittrick didn't easily forgive—or forget.

The door of the study suddenly opened, and he scowled at the young woman who stood there gazing at him nervously across the width of Chinese carpet. In a neat white blouse and slim-fitting black shirt, India's secretary was a very personable young woman, but right now her cheeks were flushed, and she was tugging anxiously at a strand of honey-blonde hair.

'Oh—Mr Kittrick,' she exclaimed in some confusion, 'I didn't realise anyone was in here. I was going to make sure everything was in order for when Mr Hastings arrives.'

Nathan's scowl disappeared, but he didn't stand up. 'Does Mr Hastings often use this office?'

'Oh, no.' The girl shook her head. 'India—that is, Miss Kittrick—is the only person, other than your father, who's used the office on a regular basis. But when...when Mr Hastings came to—to read the will...'

'He read it in here,' Nathan finished for her blandly. 'All right. I get the picture. So—do you want me to move out?'

'Of course not.' If anything, the girl looked even more embarrassed. 'Er—can I get you any coffee or anything? Mr Hastings won't be here for another hour at least.'

Nathan frowned, realising he hadn't eaten a thing since dinner the night before. And then Adele's company had prevented him from enjoying the meal. That, and India's presence at the table across the way.

'Do you think you could get me a roll as well as some coffee?' he asked, his features softening as they rested on the girl's anxious face. 'I'd be very grateful—Linda, isn't it?' And at her nod, 'If you have the time, of course.'

'No problem.' Her relief was evident, and she smiled as she backed out of the door. 'Oh—by the way, shall I tell India where you are? I think she was looking for you earlier.'

'Was she?' Nathan was surprised. After last night, he'd have thought he was the last person India would want to see. But what the hell, who could understand women? 'Sure. Why not?' he conceded, cynically. 'Perhaps you'd better bring coffee for two.'

He was standing by the long windows looking out on to the curve of the headland when he realised he was no longer alone. One moment he was watching the blue-green waters of the Atlantic splintering on the rocks at the foot of the cliffs, and the next his attention had turned inwards, drawn by that awareness of a hostility only lightly veiled.

India, he conceded ruefully, removing the arm that had been resting against the open window, and turning to face her. Though why she should be looking at him with just that expression of disgust, when he was the one who had reason to feel cheated, he couldn't imagine.

'You bastard!' she hissed, closing the door behind her, and advancing into the room. 'Just what sort of game do you think you're playing?'

Nathan's dark brows arched. 'I beg your pardon?'

'Oh, stop it! Stop pretending you don't know what I'm talking about,' she exclaimed. 'What did you say to my mother last night? What did you do to make her even think about changing her mind about you?'

Nathan's eyes narrowed. 'I gather you've spoken to your mother this morning.'

'Of course I've spoken to her.' India's eyes were dark and stormy. 'My God, wasn't it enough that you tried to seduce me? Did you have to prove your masculinity by doing what you tried to do years ago?'

'Now, wait a minute...'

Nathan's initial reaction to her appearance had surprised him. He had thought he'd want to strangle her. It was certainly how he'd felt the night before. When he'd walked into Adele's bedroom and realised what India had done, he'd felt capable of murder. But this morning the sight of her pale, worried features had disarmed him. He'd actually been halfway to finding excuses for her—until she'd started accusing him.

'Do you deny going into my mother's room?' she interrupted him, and he shook his head.

'No——'

'I thought not.'

India's generous mouth curled, and, although he knew he ought to be concentrating on his own defence, Nathan's eyes were drawn to the full breasts straining against the white silk of her vest. She was dressed this morning in the same outfit she had been wearing when she had come to meet him from the plane, and the undoubted agitation of her emotions was showing itself in the unguarded arousal of her body. It reminded him of that scene the night before, when she had been as aroused as he was. Or at least, that had been his assumption. Subsequent events had leant some doubts to his supposition...

'What did you think you'd achieve?' she was demanding now, and, pulling himself back from the brink of personal disaster, he forced himself to think coherently.

'Hey, lady, you sent me in there,' he reminded her, leaving the window to approach the desk. 'I could ask *you* what you'd been hoping to achieve. Does—Mummy—know that you extended the invitation?'

'I did not——'

'Oh, yes, you did.' Nathan rested the flat of his hands on the desk, and stared steadily at her. 'And if you didn't, you know what they call girls like you.'

'It wasn't like that.'

'It was exactly like that.'

'You tricked me.'

'*I* tricked *you*?' Nathan gazed at her disparagingly. 'You got cold feet, India; admit it. You and I both know how you really felt when I touched you.'

'No——'

'Yes.' He straightened. 'If anyone has any room for complaint here, it's me.'

India's fists clenched. 'It shouldn't have happened.'

'At last we agree on something.'

'What do you mean?' Her eyes were suspicious.

'What do you think I mean?' Nathan controlled the urge to take hold of her and force her to acknowledge she had felt something for him the night before. 'I'm not interested in your mother, India. I was never interested in your mother. Only you and my father were too blind, or too frightened, to admit it.'

India gave him a scornful look. 'How can you say a thing like that?'

Nathan's patience thinned. 'Why wouldn't I?'

'After what happened last night——'

'What the hell happened last night?' Nathan swore. 'I spent a half-hour on the beach, letting you make a damn fool of me, and then, following your directions, I walked dumbly into your mother's bedroom. What do you think happened then? Did she tell you I flung her on the bed and had my evil way with her?'

'No!'

'You surprise me.'

'Don't you dare speak about my mother like that.'

'Why not?' Nathan was too angry to be tactful. 'Believe me, India, I've got nothing to thank that woman for.'

'So why didn't you just turn around and walk out of her room immediately?' India held up her head. 'If you feel so strongly about her, how come you—you apologised?'

'The hell I did!' Nathan scowled.

'So you didn't?'

Nathan's jaw compressed. The hell of it was that he *had* apologised—though not for the reasons Adele had evidently given her daughter. He hadn't called Adele's bluff, because he'd known how unpredictable she could be. He'd been all too aware of the precariousness of his relationship with India. The last thing he'd wanted was Adele spreading her lies, and ruining his chances of convincing India of his innocence.

'All right,' he said, through clenched teeth. 'I apologised——'

'You—you——'

'For the way I'd behaved earlier in the evening,' he appended swiftly. 'God, what else was I supposed to do?

Tell her that I'd thought it was your room? That you were expecting me?'

'No...'

'Then what? Just what did *you* hope would happen?'

India swallowed. 'I didn't hope anything would happen. I...oh, if you must know, I did intend to trick you. But not—not into going into my mother's room. Never that.'

Nathan came round the desk. 'Go on.'

India lifted her shoulders. 'There's nothing much to go on with. I—my mother's windows were closed when I got to my room. I never dreamt...'

'That she might leave them open,' Nathan finished for her drily. 'So it wasn't a deliberate ploy to get me to betray myself? You weren't expecting your mother to come charging out of her room, crying rape?'

India caught her breath. 'Of course not.'

Nathan shrugged. 'And you didn't know anything about it until this morning?'

'No.'

He halted, a hand's breadth from her, looking down at her with dark, assessing eyes. He guessed she would have liked to back off, but her determination to show him that she was indifferent to his nearness kept her where she was. And he believed her. About what had happened the night before, at least. The bright wave of colour that had invaded her throat just above her collarbone and was extending over the creamy skin with the speed of summer lightning convinced him of that. She was too indignant to dissemble, too defensive of her mother to involve her unnecessarily.

And her vulnerability was irresistible. Although he knew this was neither the time nor the place to touch her, he couldn't help himself. Lifting his hand, he stroked his knuckles over the tight bud of her nipple clearly outlined against the thin cotton of her bra. With unhurried deliberation, he teased that tender nub of flesh, and when she jerked back in panic he captured her slim hips and brought her against him.

He'd forgotten he was wearing shorts until her slender legs brushed against his. And he was glad that, in those early hours of the morning when he hadn't been able to sleep, he'd taken the time to shower and shave. Her cheek was too soft to abrade with his overnight beard, and there was something decidedly erotic in feeling her bare skin against his own. In spite of her resistance, he eased one thigh between her legs, feeling the tight heat of her riding against his hairy flesh. It made him want to do more than simulate his possession, even if his tongue in her mouth was a potent compensation.

One hand cupped her head as his mouth slanted over hers, searching, and seeking, and finding the hot response he had sought the night before. Against her will it might be, he thought, but she couldn't hide the sensual hunger of her lips. Was it just that she was inexperienced? Was it his own overwhelming conceit that was convincing him of her arousal? Or did she know exactly what she was doing as she clutched the faded denim at his waist? All he did know was that she was suddenly soft, and yielding, and that his cut-offs were much too tight...

Then the door opened without warning, and India's secretary started confidently into the room. 'Coffee for two and rolls for one,' she was saying, her eyes on the bone-china cream jug she was adjusting on the tray. 'And I thought you might like some cinnamon—oh, God! I'm sorry!'

Her embarrassment was almost comical, and in other circumstances India might have made a joke of it. After all, Linda Miller had been with her for the past four years, ever since India had left school and started working for her father. They were much of an age, and friends as well as employer and employee. There was little Linda didn't know about India's life, and until recently they had often shared confidences.

But since the reading of her stepfather's will, since she had learned that Nathan might be coming back to the island, India had been much less forthcoming. That segment of her life was something she had never shared with Linda, or with anyone else, and, although she was sure her secretary must have heard the old story and been aware of the rumours that had been circulating since the reading of Aaron's will, she hadn't mentioned anything about it. For which India had been grateful—until now.

To her relief, Nathan responded much more quickly to the situation, releasing her without undue haste, and putting the solid width of her stepfather's desk between them. But perhaps he'd had to, she reflected tensely, remembering the hard heat of his body throbbing against her stomach. Dear God, he was probably used to dealing with this kind of a situation. It wasn't the first time he'd been caught in—*in flagrante delicto*, wasn't that how they put it? And how had it happened? After the night before, she should have been on her guard. But the trouble was that when he touched her she had the utmost difficulty holding on to her reason. He was handsome, and sexy, and he knew exactly how to overload her senses. Was that what he'd done to her mother? Was still doing, if what her mother had said was true.

If?

She brought herself up short at that point. Of course what Adele had said was true. She wasn't starting to doubt her own mother, was she? My God, just because Nathan looked like a devil and kissed like an angel, was she actually questioning something that had done more than anything to colour all their lives? *No*! It simply wasn't going to happen.

'Just put the tray on the desk, Linda.' Nathan's voice was calm and unemotional, the rueful grin he cast in her secretary's direction guaranteed to melt an iceberg in winter. 'Will you let us know when Mr Hastings gets here?'

'Sure thing, Mr Kittrick.'

Linda's relief was palpable, and after setting the tray on the desk she started towards the door. But she cast a doubtful look in India's direction as she did so, and, realising she had to say something, India summoned an appealing smile.

'I'll speak to you later,' she offered, hoping the other girl would get the message underlying her words. 'Thanks.'

Linda arched brows that were several shades darker than her hair in a gesture that seemed to mark her understanding, but, with the door closed behind her, India knew she had more to worry about than her secretary's curiosity. Nathan was still standing behind the desk watching her, and she mentally squared her shoulders before moving forward to take the chair across from him. In all honesty, she knew she needed the support the chair offered, and although Nathan didn't immediately follow her example she sensed he was gauging her reasons for staying.

'All right,' he said at last, and, much to her relief, he resumed his seat. 'Why don't we talk about it?'

India caught her breath. 'Talk about what?'

'Well, not the damn coffee, that's for sure,' he snarled as she gazed at him with troubled eyes. 'Let's talk about your mother, India. And about what really happened eight years ago.'

'I know what really happened.'

'No, you don't.'

'I don't want to talk about that.'

'Well, I do.' Nathan leaned towards her. 'Dammit, India, even a condemned man gets a hearing!'

'You had a hearing,' said India evenly, tearing her eyes away, and reaching for the tray. 'I—I suggest we have some coffee, and try to behave like civilised people. Mr Hastings and—and my mother will be here soon. Perhaps we should talk about the hotel.'

'To hell with the hotel!' Nathan's tone was savage. 'You burst in here, prepared to accuse me of God knows what, and you expect us just to sit here, drinking coffee, as if nothing had happened!'

'Oh, please . . .' Steeling her hands not to shake, India poured two cups of the aromatic brew. 'Haven't we talked about it enough? I—I explained what happened last night.'

'*You* explained,' he agreed harshly. 'And *I* listened. Don't I deserve the same privilege?'

'There's nothing to talk about.'

'The hell there isn't.' Nathan's chair slammed back against the bookshelves behind him, and, getting to his feet, he strode violently about the room. 'Damn, India, doesn't it occur to you that my father might have had his suspicions? Why else did he leave this place to me?'

'I—don't know. Perhaps he thought it needed a man's hand.' India put both her hands round the cup of coffee, gaining some comfort from the warmth that invaded her fingers. It was ridiculous feeling cold, with the temperature outside rising into the high seventies. 'Nathan, please—sit down.'

He didn't answer her, but she became aware that he had come to stand directly behind her chair. She couldn't see him, but she could feel him, the heat and aggression emanating from him enveloping her in its volatile cloud.

And then, as if mastering whatever demons had possessed him, he spoke. 'So,' he said softly, and it took every bit of will-power she had to prevent herself from turning and looking up at him, 'are you prepared to love me, warts and all?'

Love him?

India's mouth dried as the memory of the involuntary admission she'd made the afternoon he'd returned came back to haunt her. How could she *love* him? She didn't even know him any more.

'I—don't think you expect an answer to that,' she conveyed at last, taking too large a mouthful of her coffee, and scalding her mouth. She gasped. 'Damn!'

'Why shouldn't I expect an answer?'

Behind her, he was unaware of her discomfort, and she felt tears of frustration burn behind her eyes. 'Nathan—this is silly!'

'I agree.'

His voice had deepened, and as she groped for a tissue to dab her lips she felt his finger probing a path along her spine, from her hairline at the back, to the low neckline of her vest. Even that tenuous contact was enough to set all her nerves on edge, and she jack-knifed out of the chair as if he had attacked her.

'Stop it!' she cried, dismayed to find her voice was as unsteady as she was. 'Just—stop it, will you? When...when I said I loved you, I meant—as a brother. As the brother you used to be. I did think of you that way. You know that. But—but since you got back——'

'I've started treating you as a woman——'

'You've ruined everything,' she contradicted him tremulously, wrapping her arms across her midriff. 'You...you seem to think you can treat me like...like some kind of—sex object. I won't be used like that, Nathan. I'm not a child any more.'

'Haven't I just said that?' he put in mildly, but she ignored him.

'Since—since you went away, I've changed. I've made my own life, my own friends,' she continued urgently. 'You can't just come back here and behave as if nothing had happened, as if you can take up where . . . where you left off.'

'Did I say I wanted to?'

India groaned. 'Will you listen to me?'

'I am listening.'

'But are you taking it in?' She sighed. 'Nathan, whatever you say, whatever you think, it's too late to pretend you can change the way you are. Oh——' she spread her hands now '—I don't deny you're an attractive man——'

'Gee, thanks.'

'Or that you've probably known more women than I could even imagine——'

'Don't count on it.'

'But making love to me——'

'We haven't made love, India.'

'—is not going to change my mind about you. Don't you see? You're only proving that what everyone thinks is true!'

Nathan's scowl was back. 'Rubbish,' he said succinctly, but, before he could expand on that hypothesis, there was a tentative tap at the door. 'Come in.'

It was Linda again, popping her head round the door to announce that Mr Hastings was in Reception. 'Shall I ask him to wait?' she suggested, looking from one to the other with uneasy eyes. 'I could get him some coffee. If—if you need a little longer.'

'That won't be necessary,' replied Nathan smoothly, returning to his position behind the desk, and tapping an impatient finger against the papers he had left there. 'Show him in, Linda. And ask Mrs Kittrick to join us.'

CHAPTER EIGHT

FORTY minutes later, India was perched on the window-ledge, gazing blankly at the man she had used to regard as a brother. She wasn't alone in her scrutiny. Her mother and Arnold Hastings were similarly intent. Only Nathan seemed indifferent to the import of the news he had just delivered—or perhaps he was just faking his reaction. Surely even he must realise that the kind of money he said they needed couldn't be found in time.

Arnold Hastings was the first to recover his speech. 'But surely Aaron...' He broke off frustratedly, as if impatient with himself for sounding so indecisive, and then continued, 'Your father had accountants, Mr Kittrick. Financial advisers. I'm sure if there had been any question of a crisis they would have told him. I can't believe a man as shrewd as I always believed—as I still believe—your father was would allow himself to drift towards bankruptcy.'

'*Bankruptcy*!' Adele's horrified exclamation echoed round the room. 'You can't be serious, Arnold, surely?'

'Well——' Hastings licked his thin lips '—if what your stepson says is true——'

'What does he know?' Adele was beyond caring what anyone thought of her reaction. 'He's only been here five minutes. Just because he's got someone to pull out a handful of figures that I doubt he understands, we're all supposed to believe the resort is in imminent danger of collapse! Why—it's ludicrous! We're fully booked for the rest of the year. We're actually turning would-be visitors away. Tell him, India. Isn't that so? We've never been busier.'

Avoiding Nathan's faintly mocking gaze, India turned to the lawyer. 'Er—that is true, Mr Hastings,' she agreed, gripping the ledge at either side of her taut body with nervous fingers. 'I—I can show you the schedules.'

'They prove nothing,' put in Nathan shortly, before Hastings could reply. 'I'm not denying that the hotel attracts visitors, India. Or that the service you've been offering is anything less than unique. What I am saying—not very convincingly, apparently—is that we can't go on offering the same kind of service unless we expand.'

'Become a holiday camp, you mean?' Adele was scathing. 'Have our name scored across a dozen package-tour brochures?' She snorted. 'Our guests come here to get away from their public image. If we fill the place up with tourists, we'll lose our exclusivity.'

'Not necessarily——'

'We couldn't do it anyway,' murmured India, barely audibly. Even if she wasn't an architect, she had a little idea of what such a project would cost. 'We don't have the accommodation.'

'We could have.' Nathan had heard her, and, tipping his chair on to its back legs, he regarded her intently. 'As I said, in the short term, another wing should do it. Thirty more rooms, and we'd be viable. Fifty, and we'd turn a healthy profit.'

India looked away, incapable of withstanding his smug complacency. He must know they had no chance of rescuing the hotel. Was this his way of warning them he'd be putting the hotel on the market?

'There must be an alternative.'

Arnold Hastings was regarding Nathan earnestly as he spoke, and India wondered why he was so prepared to accept her stepbrother's assessment of the situation before her own. Of course, he knew that, whatever happened, Nathan would be making the decisions from now on. They—that was, she and her mother—were only here on sufferance. All the same...

'One alternative—if you want to call it that—is to make a balloon increase in the tariffs,' replied Nathan drily. 'And, quite honestly, I can't see anyone going for that. The original estimates may have been way out of line, but no one's going to give us a hand-out just because we made a mistake. In my experience, people who've made it didn't get that way by squandering their money.'

'And, of course, you'd know all about people like that,' exclaimed Adele scornfully. 'Arnold——' she turned to the other man '—why don't you get in touch with the accountants in London? If there is a problem—and I'm not convinced there is—I'm sure they'll be able to clear it up.'

'Oh, my dear...' Hastings's thin, ascetic features took on a thread of colour. 'I'm afraid that wouldn't do any good.'

'Why not?'

'Well, the figures——'

'The figures!' Adele glared at him. 'My God, Arnold, you're not telling me you're actually going to accept the word of a man who knows absolutely nothing about the hotel business, are you?'

'Knows nothing?'

Hastings echoed her words in evident confusion, and India wondered exactly what Nathan had told him. But, whatever it was, the lawyer must know her mother was telling the truth. However much Nathan had known of his father's affairs before he had left the island, he could have no real conception of the hotel's potential now.

'I know enough,' inserted Nathan swiftly, successfully cutting off any further comment the lawyer had been about to make. 'I've—worked in hotels. And I can read a balance sheet, believe it or not.'

Adele looked furious, but it was Hastings's expression that interested India most. He seemed totally dumbfounded, his thin, sinewy frame fairly quivering with some emotion he was having to contain. But why? What had Nathan said to evoke such a reaction? And why was he staring at her stepbrother as if imploring him to put him out of his misery?

'Arnold!' Adele hadn't given up. 'There must be something we can do.'

'There is.' But it was Nathan who answered her. 'Build a new wing.'

'What with?' It was India who spoke now. 'Is this your way of telling us you're going to have to sell the hotel to get the money?'

'No...'

'Mr Kittrick.' Hastings drew out a white handkerchief, and dabbed his perspiring brow beneath his thinning fringe of hair. 'Am I to understand that you intend to finance this development yourself?'

'He's probably going to mortgage the property,' muttered Adele bitterly. 'As if he needed an excuse.'

'As a matter of fact, there are two mortgages riding on the hotel already,' declared Nathan evenly, and India's lips parted.

'Two?' she choked.

'Yes.' Nathan's eyes were distant now as they rested upon her. 'I guess you could say Dad knew exactly what was going on.'

'Then why didn't he tell us?' demanded Adele shrilly. 'My God, this is worse, far worse, than even I imagined! If it weren't for the insurance——'

'It's far worse than any of us imagined, Mother,' said India quietly, hoping Adele wouldn't say anything else. At times like these, her mother was inclined to look for scapegoats, and she could guess Nathan's reaction if she started blaming his father. She licked her dry lips. 'So what do we do...?' She stopped and amended that. 'I mean—what are you going to do?'

'I've told you.' Nathan was infuriatingly unconcerned. 'Build a new wing. At present estimates, I'd say a couple of million should cover it.'

'A couple of million!' India knew an uncontrollable desire to laugh, only it wasn't funny. It wasn't funny at all. 'And—and how do you propose to lay your hands on that kind of money?'

'Well, let me see...'

Nathan steepled his fingers, his brows descending, as if in contemplation, but India knew his hesitation was deliberate. He was just playing with them, she thought incredulously, prolonging the suspense, when something told her he knew exactly how he was going to raise the money. And although on the one hand she was relieved, on the other she was anxious. She could see no legitimate way of acquiring such a large sum, not unless he intended turning the foyer into a casino.

And, before he could continue, her mother broke in. 'I know,' she exclaimed, staring at Nathan as she did so, and India was disturbed to see a look of consternation flit briefly over his lean face. 'It's drugs, isn't it?' Adele added. 'You said you'd spent some time in Central America. You're going to get the money from some Columbian consortium, some group who want to use the island as a stepping-stone into the States!'

The silence that followed this accusation was only significant for its embarrassment. No one, least of all India, could believe that her mother actually meant what she said. And, for all his earlier tension, Nathan's amused reaction was barely suppressed.

'Hey, I never thought of that,' he exclaimed, his obvious good humour bringing a relieved smile to Arnold

Hastings's lips. 'I wonder how I can get in touch with them. Put an ad in the paper, do you think? Or fly down to Bogota and put the word around?'

Adele looked disgruntled, but India guessed she was relieved that Nathan had taken it in good part. All the same, that still left the problem of how they were going to raise the money, and, for all Nathan's mocking banter, there was a lot at stake.

'Are you thinking of offering—shares in the hotel?' India ventured stiffly, in an effort to shift attention from her mother, and Nathan's eyes moved to Arnold Hastings.

'I don't somehow think you'd get many takers,' he remarked, as the older man fidgeted with his briefcase. 'Isn't that right, Hastings? People usually want to see a return on their investment.'

'Well, yes...'

'Then what are you going to do?' demanded Adele. 'India's right. If there's no money for expansion, you'll have to sell—eventually.'

'I didn't say there was no money,' Nathan corrected her blandly. He continued to look at Hastings. 'Isn't that right, Arnold? At no time did I imply that the situation was hopeless.'

'Then why don't you tell us what you're going to do?' asked Adele tersely, and India's nerves tightened as Nathan turned to her mother again.

'I'm prepared to invest some of my own money—if the conditions are right.'

'*You*!'

Both India and her mother said the word in unison, though India's wasn't audible, just a framing of her lips.

'Yes, me,' agreed Nathan, lowering his hands to the desk and regarding all of them with an air of satisfaction. 'Providing we can agree on the development, along the lines I've suggested, and India is prepared to stay on as social director.'

India climbed off her bicycle, and wheeled it off the road into the sand-dunes. Below her, the untouched expanse of Abalone Cove lay silent in the afternoon heat. Apart from a couple of sand-crabs, scrabbling anxiously out of her way, the cove was deserted. At this hour of the afternoon, even the birds were absent, returning again in the early evening, when the incoming tide brought flotsam on to the beach.

But for now she had the place to herself, and she kicked off her canvas boots, and slip-slid down on to the sand. She left her bicycle hidden in a mound of coarse grass, knowing, from previous experience, that no one would disturb it there.

Indeed, she doubted many people knew of the cove's existence. It was well hidden, and far away from Abaco Bay and its more civilised environs; the northern end of the island was virtually untouched and remote. Without Nathan's guidance, she would never have known it was there. As a girl alone, she would never have wandered so far from the grounds of the hotel.

But Nathan had brought her here many times, and these days she was confident enough to come on her own. After all, its very privacy ensured her safety. And besides, there were no would-be rapists on Pelican Island.

Finding a suitable spot, she put down the small rucksack she was carrying. Inside were two cans of Coke, stored in an insulated bag to keep them cold, and her towel. Nothing else, apart from a comb, and the silky green bra of her bikini.

She stood for several minutes, just staring at the view. There was nothing like it, she thought, watching the translucent green water turn to curls of lace on the beach. Just sun, and sea, and the distant sound of the surf breaking over Cat Point half a mile away. No parasols, no club chairs, no people. Heaven!

Peeling off her shorts, she glanced round before taking off her cotton T-shirt. It wasn't that she expected that anyone might see her. It was just an automatic reflex, but one that she couldn't quite throw off. However, the only sign of human life was a sail on the horizon, too far away to bother her or interfere with her isolation.

Nevertheless, a shiver feathered down her spine, in spite of the noon heat. For once, she wasn't quite as relaxed as she usually was, and she had no trouble in finding the cause. It was Nathan, of course. Nathan—and his unnerving plans for her future. How could he finance the kind of development he was talking about? And how could she remain on the island when she couldn't even trust him?

Trying not to think about it, she padded down the beach and into the water. She didn't hurry. She liked to prolong the moment before she plunged into the waves. It felt so deliciously cool, against skin that was hot from her exertions. Her mother always thought she was mad for going cycling when the sun was at its zenith.

But it was a period of the day that India considered peculiarly her own. The guests were enjoying lunch on the terrace, and it was too early to start thinking about dinner. And, after spending much of the morning in her office, she felt entitled to an hour devoted only to herself.

At least she hadn't had to worry about seeing Nathan for the past few days. The morning after that interview with Arnold Hastings he had left for the mainland, ostensibly to consult with his own financial advisers. Though who they were, and what they were consulting about, India could only guess.

It was all so unsatisfactory, not knowing what was going to happen, where he was going to get the money from. She couldn't believe Nathan had that kind of capital to play with. What had he said? A couple of million? Dollars or pounds, it didn't seem to make a lot of difference. She had never handled that kind of money, and, although she had known the hotel was worth much more than that, it was a nebulous amount, and one she had never expected to realise.

But, she had to admit, Nathan had seemed quite at home with the figures. And, remembering the look that had crossed Mr Hastings's face, she suspected he knew more than he was saying, too. It reminded her of that comment Senator Markham had made, about that land he owned in Arizona. Did they know something she and her mother should know? Had Mr Hastings discovered something else when he'd been making his investigations into Nathan's whereabouts?

But why should he tell them? India grimaced, and, abandoning her unhappy reflections, she dived into the deepening waves. It was probably as she had thought. Arnold Hastings was a shrewd organiser, and he wasn't likely to betray the confidences of a man who could find a million dollars at a moment's notice.

The water was cooler than she had anticipated. Or perhaps she had been standing in the sun too long. In any event, it briefly took her breath away, and she came up pedalling her legs, and gasping for air. Damn, she thought, as her heart raced, and her lungs pumped urgently in her chest. She was letting this affair with Nathan get to her. There was nothing she could do, so why didn't she just put it out of her mind?

Because of her mother, she conceded with a sigh, as her brain cleared. Ever since that morning, Adele had talked of little else, and for once India's patience with her mother was wearing thin. It wasn't as if Adele had anything to gain by staying on the island. But she was insistent that India should accept Nathan's offer, and ensure their immediate future at least. She doubted her mother really believed that Nathan still had any affection for her. Despite what she had implied to the contrary, his attitude that morning had not been that of a lover. No, whatever his feelings had been, they appeared to have been shredded by the passage of time, and only his bitterness remained. A bitterness hardened by his father's death, she acknowledged ruefully. If only he could have spoken to Aaron before he'd died...

She felt a little better as she swam back to the shore. Nathan had said she could have some time to think over his offer, and until he came back from the mainland it was not a problem she needed to face. After all, it could be days—weeks—before he got back. Surely finding the kind of money he was talking about was not going to be that easy?

She walked out of the shallows, squeezing water from her hair. She had drawn it back with an elasticated band before she'd been swimming, but now she released the band, and ran her fingers through its length, drawing it forward over her shoulders to dry in the sun.

And then she saw him. He was stretched out on the sand, right beside her rucksack, her towel resting casually across his thigh. He was propped up on his elbows, one leg outstretched, the other bent at the knee, wearing only cut-off denims and an inscrutable expression.

Her heart palpitated rapidly, and she was instantly conscious of her semi-nudity. Thankfully, her hair was long, and did a modestly successful job of providing a screen, but her breasts had been stimulated by the water, and refused to stay out of sight.

If only she had taken the towel with her, or, alternatively, worn the bikini bra that was in her rucksack. No one, not even Steve Whitney, had caught her in such an embarrassing position, and she could tell by the narrowing of his eyes that her appearance had been noticed.

She halted several feet from him, digging her toes into the hot sand, and feeling her shoulders prickling with the heat. Only it wasn't just the heat, she admitted tensely. The sun wasn't causing the warmth that pooled in the pit of her stomach.

Summoning as much composure as she possessed, she nodded towards the towel lying on his leg. 'Would you mind?'

Nathan glanced down at the towel. Then he looked up again. 'Do you usually go swimming like that?' he enquired briefly.

India caught back the indignant retort that sprang to her lips. 'When I'm alone,' she replied pointedly. 'Now, if you'd——'

'And what if someone else decided to join you?' he cut in. 'What then?'

'That's not very likely. No one knows about this cove, except...' The 'you' hovered unspoken. 'Nathan, please...'

'Please what?' He pushed himself into an upright position, and looked up at her with dark, enquiring eyes. He knew exactly what she wanted, damn him, but he was going to make her say it, beg him to hand her the towel.

'I'd like to get dry,' she said tautly, crossing her arms over her body, and gripping her shoulders with stiff fingers. 'If you don't mind.'

'And if I do?'

'Nathan, why are you doing this?'

He shrugged his broad, muscled shoulders, brown shoulders that gleamed dully in the brilliant light. 'Perhaps I'm just trying to prove how unwise it is for you to go swimming alone in such isolated surroundings,' he remarked idly. 'Does anyone know where you are?'

India's stomach hollowed. 'My mother knows I've gone cycling,' she said quickly.

'Big deal.' Nathan was unimpressed. 'Anyone else?'

India calculated the risks of pretending she had told Steve about her hide-away, and then dismissed the thought. Steve didn't know about Abalone Cove, and she didn't want him to. Besides, Nathan was just being annoying. Why should she play his game by being defensive?

'Just give me the towel,' she said flatly. 'I have to get back.'

'OK.'

With a lithe movement, Nathan came to his feet. But, instead of throwing her the towel, he brought it to her, shaking it out as he did so.

'Thank you, that's far enough,' she exclaimed, reaching for it with some relief. But Nathan ignored her outstretched hand, and, side-stepping the barrier, he wrapped the towel around her from behind.

The initial gratitude she felt at being able to cover herself was short-lived, however, Nathan didn't step back after winding the towel about her. His arms remained around her, and her pulses raced when his hands began to knead the cloth against her. With a growing sense of panic, she realised he was drying her himself, his knuckles brushing the undersides of her breasts as he rubbed her midriff.

Her withdrawal was instinctive, but her movements were sluggish, her senses drugged by the seductive movement of his hands. She knew she had to stop him before her emotions betrayed her, but it all seemed to be happening in slow motion, and it was difficult to find the words.

'No,' she got out at last, trying to press his hands away from her. 'Nathan, you mustn't.'

'Why mustn't I?' he asked softly, ignoring her plea in any case, and continuing his disturbing siege of her senses. 'You wanted to get dry, didn't you? What's the matter? Aren't I doing a good job?'

Too good a job, she thought unsteadily, as his probing hands moved down, over her flat stomach. And he wasn't making her dry, she realised, shivering in the heat. There were parts of her body that were getting very wet.

'Nathan, stop it,' she choked, the words dragged up from the very depths of her being. 'You can't do this. It isn't right.'

'It feels right to me,' he retorted, using the ends of the towel to dry her hair. His hands brushed over her shoulders. 'Hey, baby, you've got the softest skin.'

He hadn't touched her breasts yet, but he was going to. And, God help her, she was beginning to wish he would. Every inch of her skin tingled with that wareness, and the heat coming from his body at her back enveloped her in his male fragrance.

But, before his hands slid from her shoulders, he dipped his head, and she felt his tongue moving against the side of her neck. His hair fell forward, warm and vital against her cheek, and her breathing felt suspended.

'Nathan...' she moaned, but he wasn't listening to her. Like her, he seemed lost in a world of his own making, and the words he uttered defied her resistance.

'Do you know, I've thought about doing this ever since that night you sent me into your mother's room,' he told her roughly, and she uttered a tremulous protest.

'I—I didn't send you into my mother's room...'

'It seemed that way to me.'

'No.' She caught her breath as he drew the towel aside and his thumbs rubbed sensuously along the sides of her breasts. 'That is, I didn't—know her windows would be open.'

'But you did set me up, right?' he reminded her softly, his tormenting caress driving her almost insane with longing. Why didn't he touch the hard peaks of her breasts? They were aching for him to do so, and it was only with a supreme effort of will that she stopped herself from dragging his hands to them.

'I—I...couldn't handle it,' she got out unsteadily. She shook her head helplessly. 'Nathan——'

'Shut up,' he breathed huskily, and to her intense relief his palms scraped over her throbbing nipples. Then, before she had time to wallow in the sensation, he twisted her round in his arms and found her mouth with his.

Her breasts were against his chest now, crushed against the muscled expanse of his sweat-slicked body. The fine covering of coarse hair that thickened between his pectoral muscles and arrowed down below the low waistband of his cut-offs was rough against her softness, but she didn't care. Her tingling breasts welcomed the abrasion, and her legs reacted similarly to the thrust of his hairy thighs. She felt surrounded by his masculinity, assaulted by the urgent pressure of his flesh.

But it was a tender assault, and she didn't draw back. Curiosity, hunger, *need*—or perhaps a combination of all three—made any resistance impossible. With his mouth silencing any protest she might have cared to make, a strange sense of inevitability was creeping over her. Perhaps this was what she had been born for; perhaps this was meant to be. And when she moved sinuously against him, she knew she was inviting his response.

She heard him suck in his breath when her palms slid over his rigid nipples. And there was something innately satisfying in exploring the hard strength of his body, her arms arching around his neck to bind him even closer. Her hands slid into his hair, delighting in the way the damp, silky strands clung to her fingers. Her nails raked his scalp at the back, and dug possessively into his neck.

But when his tongue plunged into her mouth, she arched against him, and felt the thickening rise of his maleness. Hard and throbbing, it strained against the uncertain barrier of his clothing, making her aware of what this was doing to him in every kind of way.

His kiss hardened, and lengthened, drugging her with its sweetness, and seducing her with its need. Her limbs felt as if they were melting, liquefying, turning her bones to water. She felt as if she were turning into a molten, fluid mass.

He groaned, and the sound echoed in her head with a persistent toll. Deep, and anguished, it reverberated throughout her system, inciting an answering sigh that gushed softly into his mouth.

He seemed to shudder, and his hands moved from the provocative curve of her hips to the thrusting swell of her breasts. With infinite care, he cupped their luscious fullness, and lifted them deliberately to his mouth. Then, with studied sensuality, he caressed each one with his tongue, causing a flame of fire to leap through her.

Her shocked, 'Oh, God!' seemed to please him, and a curious expression crossed his dark face. Then, when she was panting for him to go on, to take her nipples into his mouth, and do whatever he wanted with her, he let her go. Pushing her gently but firmly away from him, he bent and picked up her towel. 'Better finish drying yourself,' he advised her, running a rather rueful hand over the swelling in his denims. 'You don't want to catch cold.'

CHAPTER NINE

WELL, she'd called him a bastard, and now he was one, Nathan thought grimly, sliding behind the wheel of the beach buggy he'd driven to the cove. So what if the success of his mission didn't fill him with the satisfaction he'd expected? He'd paid her back, hadn't he? He'd made her feel a little of the frustration he'd felt when she'd run out on him. And if the wounded expression in her eyes was going to haunt him for countless nights to come, so be it. She deserved everything he'd given her, and maybe a little more.

Not that that made his own condition any easier to bear. It should have. But it didn't. For the second time in as many weeks, he ached with the need to make love with her. No—not make love, he corrected himself harshly, have sex. He wanted to have sex with her, and his own sex was feeling the strain.

He didn't feel a lot better when he arrived back at the hotel. Even though he'd waited, out of sight in the sand-dunes, until he'd seen she was dressed and ready to leave before driving away from the cove, he was still suffering the after-effects of his abstinence. In consequence, he was in no mood to be civil to anyone, and he strode through the hotel, and into his father's office, uncaring of the unsuitability of his appearance.

'Hey, man, didn't you find her?'

Greg Sanders looked up from the balance sheet he had been studying when Nathan burst into the room to give his friend a rueful look. In his crisp blue shirt and darker chinos, the black man could not have presented a more obvious contrast to his rumpled partner, and Nathan regarded him grudgingly before flinging himself into the chair opposite.

'Yes, I found her,' he replied shortly, crossing one ankle over his knee, and taking several steadying gulps of air. For a moment he had forgotten he had brought Greg back with him, and he stared grimly at the floor as he struggled to calm his senses.

'You want I should leave?' offered Greg after a moment, but Nathan shook his head. He had his own treacherous emotions under control again, and he offered the other man an ironic grin.

'Hell, no,' he said, and, pushing himself to his feet again, he crossed to the refrigerated cabinet hidden behind a panelled wall. 'What I want is a beer, or, better yet, a couple. How about you? Is Michelob OK?'

'Sounds good.' Greg watched his friend and partner with faintly concerned eyes. 'Did something happen?' he asked. 'Something you want to talk about?'

Nathan handed him a can of beer, and then, pulling the tab on his own, took a long, thirst-quenching swallow. Only when the alcohol was causing a warm glow to invade his belly did he look at Greg again, and then it was with a certain amount of diffidence, and a decided lacing of self-mockery.

'I guess you could say I just beat up on myself,' he remarked drily, returning his attention to the can. He grimaced. 'But what the hell! She had it coming.'

Greg frowned. 'Who are we talking about here? Your stepmother?'

'God, no!' Nathan stared at him aghast, and then, realising he wasn't making a lot of sense, he pulled a wry face. 'India. I'm talking about India.'

Greg regarded him for several seconds, and then arched an ebony brow. 'She really gets to you, doesn't she? You know, if you hadn't told me different, I'd say you were in serious trouble here.'

'With India?'

Nathan managed to sound as outraged as he felt, but deep down he wasn't so convinced. He had told Greg the story of how he and his father came to be estranged years ago, one night after they'd become partners and he'd had one too many beers. Or, at least, that was how he'd excused himself the next morning. He wasn't in the habit of confiding in anyone, and Greg had never betrayed his confidence. But now he wished he had kept his maudlin disclosures to himself. He didn't need another conscience. His own was quite enough.

'OK.' Greg held up his hand, palm outwards, in a gesture of submission. 'So what's eating you? You and she had a row, right?'

Nathan's short laugh was hardly humorous. 'You might say that,' he agreed, finishing his beer and going back for another. He endeavoured to cast off the burden of despondency that was weighing on his shoulders, and indicated the papers on the desk. 'So—what do you think about the projection?'

'You really want to talk about this now?' Greg looked doubtful.

'Why not?'

'Well—hell, I thought you might like to go take a shower,' returned his partner equably. He deliberately adopted a southern drawl, and went on, 'Ain't no law that says y'all got to gussy up for th'occasion, but man, that's the sorriest apology for a dress suit I ever did see!'

Nathan's humour was not forced this time. 'Yeah,' he said, looking down at his bare chest and sand-smeared legs. 'I guess you have a point.' He finished his second beer, and, dropping the can into the waste-bin, he sauntered to the door. 'OK, give me fifteen minutes. I'd hate to offend your sensibilities.'

He showered in the bathroom of the suite they had allotted him, changing the shabby cut-offs for a pair of black cotton trousers and a matching collarless shirt. Towelling his hair dry, he acknowledged the fact that he really would have to get it cut soon. He had never let it get so long.

Though not as long as India's, he reflected broodingly, remembering the way she'd looked when she had first come up out of the water, before she'd known anyone was watching her. She'd looked incredible, he thought unwillingly, tall, and slim, and beautiful, and utterly natural. She'd been squeezing the water from her hair, that wonderful length of fiery hair that defied any words to describe it. She'd seemed completely indifferent to her semi-nudity, totally unaware of being observed.

And even when she had seen him, she hadn't made any coy moves to protect herself. She had let her hair do it for her. Though not very successfully, he recalled, recollecting how her breasts had played peekaboo with his senses. He'd had the devil's own job to keep his hands off her, long before he'd let his own needs almost get the better of him.

And they had almost been his undoing, he could acknowledge now. Wrapping the towel around her, drying that creamy flesh, had been the subtlest kind of torture. God, he was still tortured now, he thought, despising his treacherous emotions. He wanted her; there was no doubt about that, whatever he had said to Greg Sanders. He was infatuated with her. He had thought of little else ever since he'd returned to New York. Through all his business meetings, she had been there, seducing his mind, betraying everything he had sworn to avenge. But he could resist her. He had to. Or she'd never believe he was innocent of the crime for which he'd been condemned . . .

* * *

Nathan didn't join the guests for dinner. He and Greg had a sandwich down at the marina while he was showing the other man around, and then Greg went back to the hotel to study the figures Nathan had had prepared by his accountant in New York. Nathan's idea was that the island complex should be brought under the umbrella of Sullivan's Spas, but with provision made for it to retain its individuality. That way, he would protect his father's dream, while providing the hotel with the resources necessary to ensure its expansion.

That was why he had brought Greg back with him, why he had wanted the other man's input. He never did anything these days without consulting with Greg. Over the years, they had become quite a daunting combination, Greg's experience in practical matters vying comfortably with Nathan's entrepreneurial skills. He had needed to know what Greg thought about taking on a project that initially could prove quite a liability.

In fact, the other man had been favourably impressed with Pelican Island, and they had spent most of the afternoon discussing how it could be made viable without losing its enviable reputation. No rumours of its precarious financial situation must be allowed to reach the Press. There was nothing like news of a take-over to cause uncertainty in people's minds, and it was important that Kittrick's Hotel should maintain its present position in the ratings. Nathan was sure a rescue package could be put together, and he also knew that sooner or later he was going to have to tell India and Adele who he was.

He wasn't looking forward to it. He was reluctant to give Adele any information that she might conceivably use against him. She had already done a brilliant job of poisoning India's mind against him, and, although he didn't see how she could hurt him any more than she had already done, he didn't trust her.

After telling Greg he would see him later, Nathan decided what he'd really like to do was take the *Wayfarer* out for a sail. Aboard the old boat was the only place he really felt close to his father, and he had plans to have the craft overhauled and kept for his own personal use. It was a quixotic idea, perhaps. When the hotel was busy, all craft were kept in permanent use, and the obvious financial loss would be considerable. But this was one decision he had made without Greg's approval, though he had no doubt that his partner would have no difficulty endorsing it.

The cabin was locked, like before, but that presented no difficulties. His father had always kept a key hidden aboard the vessel, and, after removing it from its hiding-place, he descended the steps into the small saloon.

He'd brought a couple of cans of beer with him from the clubhouse, and he stowed them in the refrigerated cabinet before checking that everything was as he had left it. Evidently someone kept the old girl in order, he reflected drily, for the brasses were polished and the paintwork was gleaming.

The sound of footsteps overhead brought a frown to his lean face, and only when well-worn sneakers below grey-haired legs appeared on the stairway did his expression clear. The legs gave way to white shorts and a cotton T-shirt with the words 'Kittrick's Marina' emblazoned across the front, and Horace Williams's gnarled black face came into view.

'Hey, Nathan, is that you?' he exclaimed, a broad smile cracking his mahogany features. 'I heard you were back.'

'None other,' said Nathan, shaking the other man's hand. 'How've you been, Horace? It's good to see a familiar face.'

'Yes.' Horace looked a little rueful now. 'There's not a lot of us left these days. Lot of new faces around here, Nathan; a lot of new faces.'

'So I noticed.'

'Yeah, well, Ralph said he'd been talking to you. Got me in quite a state when I found the cabin unlocked the other day.'

'Sorry about that.' Nathan was apologetic. 'I just wanted to get away from—the hotel for a while.' He glanced round. 'This seemed like a good place.'

'Hmm.' Horace nodded, and scratched his head. 'Your daddy sure liked the old *Wayfarer*,' he agreed. 'Spent a lot of time down here before he died.'

'Did he?' Nathan's voice betrayed his regret. 'I wish I'd known he was ill, Horace, I really do.'

'Well, if it's any consolation, I don't think anybody knew how ill he really was,' replied Horace swiftly. 'We'd gotten so used to seeing him down here; no one really thought anything of it when he took to sleeping down here as well.'

Nathan stared at him. 'My father slept here?'

'Most times.' Horace nodded. 'Guess he didn't want to worry anyone. Must have... well...' He broke off awkwardly, and then, seeing Nathan's raised eyebrows, he finished awkwardly, 'Well, had a few disturbed nights towards—towards the end.'

'Yes.' Nathan absorbed this news with some misgivings. It was obvious his father had had a lot on his mind, and the knowledge that if he'd known he could have helped him left a nasty taste in his mouth.

'You—er—you staying?' Horace asked now. 'I don't mean down here. I mean on the island. You going to run the hotel now that your daddy's made you the main man?'

Nathan managed a small smile. 'Something like that,' he conceded wearily. 'Oh—and don't worry. I've got no plans for making any changes in the staff.' Not immediately, anyway, he added silently. It all depended on how quickly the hotel could be turned around.

'I'll be sure to pass the news.' Horace grinned, and then glanced hopefully towards the stairway. 'OK. Then I'll leave you to it. You just holler if you need anything, hear?'

Nathan nodded again, and, after another awkward pause, Horace scrambled back up the stairway. He was obviously glad to get away, and Nathan didn't blame him. There was no easy way to tell someone his father and stepmother had been as estranged as he'd suspected. It had just been Horace's bad luck to be the one to deliver the news.

Left alone, Nathan didn't immediately follow him up to the deck. The idea of taking the *Wayfarer* out had lost some of its appeal, and he flung himself on to a cushioned banquette, and gazed broodingly out of the window.

Outside, dusk was darkening the boardwalk that ran between the moored vessels, and casting shadows over the dock. Stars were beginning to appear on the horizon, and the sky was deepening to the colour of black velvet. It was all so beautiful, he thought bitterly. The kind of place most people only dreamed about. But, like all paradises, this one had its serpent and, unfortunately, his father had married it.

There was a party going on, on one of the vessels moored nearer the clubhouse. He could hear the sounds of voices and laughter, and the lilt of calypso music drifted over the water. At least some people were enjoying themselves, he reflected dourly. And, after all, that was what they came here for.

It was getting dark in the cabin, and, forcing himself to move, he switched on the lamps. Immediately the room was filled with a mellow golden glow, and, determined to dispel his melancholy, he sat down at the bureau where his father had kept all the papers pertaining to the craft.

They were hardly private papers. The bureau wasn't even locked. But Nathan still had certain reservations about going through his father's things. He had the instinctive feeling that at any moment Aaron was going to come clattering down the stairwell, demanding to know what he thought he was doing.

But, of course, no one came. The yacht remained as still and silent as before, the only sounds the persistent lap of the tide against the gunwale, and the usual creaks and groans associated with any craft.

The pockets of the bureau were filled with scraps of paper, many of them old weather reports and dates of charters, which should have been destroyed years ago. There were nautical charts, and invoices detailing what repairs had been made to the vessel, as well as wrappers from potato chips and chocolate bars, revealing that his father had often missed his meals as well.

Nathan's lips tightened as he pulled out the ship's log, and he smoothed rueful fingers over its weathered surface. Although *Wayfarer* could never be classed as an ocean-going vessel, his father had always insisted on keeping a formal record of its history, and within the book's pages were details of every trip the yacht had made. It was all there, written in his father's distinctive hand, and Nathan felt a lump invade his throat. 'Dammit, Dad,' he muttered, 'why did you have to be so stubborn?'

Some of the pages were stuck together, the result, he imagined, of a seepage of sea-water during a particularly rough passage. It was possible to capsize a boat in these waters, especially late in the year, when hurricanes came roaring up from the Caribbean. Nathan had experienced some pretty hairy passages himself, but he had always had complete faith in his father's judgement.

Now, however, he eased the pages apart, and as he did so another scrap of paper tumbled on to the desk. Not another weather report, he thought impatiently, unfolding the page. And it wasn't. It was a letter, apparently addressed to him.

His hand trembled. The handwriting was his father's again, and he wondered when he had written it. There was no date, not even a signature, but the name on the top was his. Dear God, he thought, as he tried to focus. He could so easily have missed it.

Holding it towards the lamp, he scanned the scrawled words with some misgivings. It was one thing to sort through sailing charts, and quite another to read a letter he might not have been meant to see. But his father was dead, he consoled himself. Nothing he did could hurt him now.

> Dear Nathan, if you are reading this, then I must hope that you've forgiven me. At the very least, you must have returned to the island, and by now you must know the extent of my failure.

Nathan swallowed. It was not what he had expected, and he wasn't at all sure he wanted to go on. It was obvious his father had written this after he had made his will in his favour, after he had realised the gamble wasn't going to work.

He sighed. He had to go on—if for no other reason than to satisfy his own curiosity. But God, what was Aaron asking forgiveness for? He read on.

> But the hotel isn't important. It can always be sold, and perhaps it, and the island, will realise enough to pay off its creditors. Adele will be solvent. I've made sure of that. My only regret is that India will lose

everything. She's worked so hard to make a success of this place. Poor India. She'll think I've let her down.

Nathan took a steadying breath. It was incredible. It was as if his father was there, talking to him. If only he could tell him how he felt, too.

But not as much as I've let you down, Nathan. I should have known. I should have suspected. You'd never lied to me before, but I wouldn't listen. I was besotted. A besotted old fool who couldn't see what was happening, even when it was staring me in the face. Adele will never change. I know now that one man will never be enough for her. There've been a handful of them over the years. Men she's met here and in the United States. She doesn't think I know. Or perhaps she doesn't care. Why should she? She despises me and all I stand for.

Nathan was sweating now. He could feel the beads of sweat standing out on his forehead, and the hand clenched around the sheet of paper was hot and clammy.

Anyway, it's too late now. My sins—and Adele's—will die with me. And I'm going to die. I know it. That's why I'm writing this note. Maybe one day, Nathan, you'll read this and...

But that was as far as it went. Read this, and what? Nathan thought bitterly. Understand? Forgive? *Weep*? For the first time since he had learned of his father's death, he felt the hot prick of tears behind his eyes. 'Dear God,' he groaned, thrusting the letter aside, and burying his head in his hands. Why was it always too late?

CHAPTER TEN

INDIA stood at her window, staring out into the darkness. She hadn't turned on the light, but that didn't stop the insects from hurling themselves at the glass. She knew they were attracted by the uplighters that dimly illuminated the terrace, and she was used to their nightly ritual. But it was a futile ritual, she thought wearily. Yet wasn't everything?

She sighed. That was hardly a positive thought. But then she didn't feel particularly positive this evening. In fact, she felt downright depressed, and Steve had known right away that something was wrong.

The truth was that she shouldn't have agreed to have dinner with Steve this evening, feeling as she did. She hadn't been in a good mood before she'd gone out, and the discovery that someone was aboard the *Wayfarer* had sent a shudder of apprehension streaking through her.

She had known who it was, of course. Nathan hadn't been seen since he had gone off with that other man this afternoon, and the very fact that Greg Sanders had been having a lonely drink in the bar had told its own story.

Adele had informed her that Greg Sanders had come with Nathan, and her interpretation of his presence was that he must be someone who was prepared to lend Nathan some money. Why else would Nathan have spent the afternoon showing him over the place, and why else had he been seen in Nathan's office going over the balance sheets?

And the annoying thing was that she wouldn't have known that Nathan wasn't spending the evening with him if she hadn't agreed to let Steve cook her dinner. But Steve's apartment was down at the marina, and the lights winking from the *Wayfarer* had been unmistakable. She hadn't needed Steve to point them out, and when he had she had almost bitten his head off.

Which had set the seal on the rest of the evening, she admitted, guiltily aware that she had used Steve to assuage her own frustration. He hadn't deserved her anger, but since Nathan had left her at Abalone Cove she hadn't been fit company for anyone.

And why? she asked herself disparagingly. Because Nathan had aroused feelings she'd hardly known she possessed? Because he'd played on her emotions, and left her wanting? Just as she'd left him, she conceded bitterly. And how easily she'd succumbed. *Oh, God*!

Twisting her hands together, she turned away from the windows, and paced agitatedly about the room. What was he trying to do to her? she wondered achingly. What did he really want? She didn't fool herself that he was seriously interested in her. She was sure he was only using her to bait her mother. But why? Why?

She couldn't stay here and find out. The thought came out of nowhere, but as soon as she recognised it she knew it was true. There was no way she could continue in her present position with Nathan running the hotel. No matter how painful the thought of leaving here might be, staying on was only going to be more painful in the long run.

She halted in the middle of the floor, pressing her palms to her hot cheeks. Yes, she thought unsteadily, that was the only answer. She couldn't go on working for a man who had no respect either for her or her mother. She should have realised that right from the beginning. As soon as she'd known Nathan was coming back to the island, she should have made her plans to leave.

She drew a deep breath. But what about her mother? Adele wasn't going to take her decision very happily. And it was because of Adele that she had made such a concerted effort to get on with her stepbrother, she told herself, not altogether truthfully. But anyway, that was before they had known the hotel was in financial difficulties. Who knew what might happen now?

Of course, there was still Nathan's ultimatum to deal with, his contention that he'd only rescue the hotel if she stayed on. But he couldn't honestly expect her to honour that now. Not when he had shown how little regard he had for her. No, she thought grimly. All bets were off.

Turning, she lowered her hands, and walked back to the window. She could always try to talk to Nathan, she reflected. He was probably still down at the marina. If she went and saw him now, perhaps she could explain her position. She might even be able to persuade him to let her mother stay on. What harm could it do?

She caught her lower lip between her teeth. No, she thought flatly. That wasn't a good idea. If her previous experience was anything to go on, Nathan would have been drinking, and trying to talk seriously to a man in his cups was not recommended. Or was it? She frowned. He might be easier to handle in that state. And she'd certainly make sure that what had happened this afternoon didn't happen again.

She sighed, still undecided. Common sense was telling her to wait until the morning before attempting to talk to him again. But what if she didn't see him—or not alone, anyway? Greg Sanders was here, and no doubt he'd be around any time she tried to speak to Nathan. At least she could be sure of some privacy down at the marina. Before she'd come to her room, she had seen Nathan's friend talking to Nicki in Reception.

She glanced down at what she was wearing, and then reached firmly for the buttons. The sapphire skirt and matching tunic might have been suitable for dinner with Steve, but they were certainly not suitable for what she hoped would be a business meeting. No, a plain black T-shirt dress and white deck shoes seemed infinitely less provocative, and she plaited her hair into a single braid, and slung it over her shoulder.

The fact that she now looked about sixteen was a disadvantage, but she dismissed it. It didn't matter how old she looked; it was what she had to say that was the important thing. Oh, she hoped Nathan was in a receptive frame of mind. She hoped he'd see the sense of her argument.

To her relief, she encountered no one on her trek down to the marina. People were still about, but they were either dancing at the hotel, or walking on the beach, or partying at the clubhouse. Someone was having a party on one of the yachts, and the rhythmic beat of the music hid the sound of her footsteps as she trotted along the boardwalk. So far, so good, she thought as she neared the lights of the *Wayfarer*. Nathan was still here. She just hoped he was alone.

It was impossible to board the boat without giving her presence away. Even her weight caused the yacht to rock at its moorings, and she waited, expectantly, for Nathan to come charging up from below.

But he didn't. Indeed, if the lights hadn't still been burning, she'd have had her doubts about the yacht's being occupied. Perhaps he'd just left the lights on, she thought uneasily. Or perhaps it wasn't Nathan at all.

She crossed the deck quickly, before she could have second thoughts, and, taking a determined breath, she started down the varnished stairway. It was months since she had been on board the *Wayfarer*, months since she had come here looking for Aaron. He had spent so much time at the marina, and, although she'd never thought of it before, she wondered if that was why her mother had become a seasoned traveller. It had been obvious they had had little to say to one another in recent years, but Adele had always maintained that nothing was wrong.

Before she reached the bottom of the stairs, India ducked her head to peer into the cabin. And her breath escaped with a rush. Nathan was there, stretched out on the banquette, but his eyes were closed.

Was he asleep? With some misgivings, India came down the final few steps, watching him all the time. But he didn't move. He just lay there, on his back, his shirt riding up above his midriff, the waistband of his trousers unbuttoned and gaping open.

She sucked in her breath at the sight of the dark hair that nestled in that provocative opening, and then tore her eyes away. She wasn't supposed to be here. She certainly wasn't supposed to see him like this, one arm shading his eyes, one foot sprawled on the floor. His other foot rested on the banquette, his knee updrawn, and absurdly vulnerable.

She took another fluttering gulp of air, and trod softly across the floor. If he was asleep, she was going to have to abandon her ideas of talking to him tonight. And, perhaps that was just as well, she conceded, as her eyes drifted over him again. Apart from one empty can of beer, crushed and lying on the carpet, there was no evidence that he had been doing any serious drinking, and she wondered if that night on the terrace had been the exception rather than the rule. After all, he didn't look as if he imbibed very freely. His torso was as lean and hard as an athlete's. In fact it was that, as much as anything Adele had said, that had persuaded her that he must have spent the last eight years in some manual occupation.

So what was she doing? she asked herself, as she stood uncertainly beside the bunk. He was asleep. He wasn't faking. So why didn't she get out of there now, at once, before he woke up and decided she had been spying on him?

Because she didn't want to, she admitted unwillingly. Not yet. There was something almost illicit about standing there, watching him as he slept, and she was loath to give it up. Besides, it was the first time since he had come back to the island that she had been able to look at him unobserved, and it was too good an opportunity to miss.

And then she frowned, as she noticed something she hadn't noticed before. There were stains on his cheeks, smears, as if he had rubbed his face with a grubby hand. Rubbed away *tears*, she realised incredulously. Dear God, Nathan had been crying!

She glanced round and saw her stepfather's leather-bound notebook lying open on the bureau. Nathan must have been reading the notebook, she thought, biting her lip. Seeing his father's handwriting again must have affected him more than she'd have thought.

The realisation should have had her heading for the stairs at a rush. If there was one thing guaranteed to add to Nathan's resentment of her voyeurism, it was the knowledge that she had seen him helpless and vulnerable. He wouldn't forgive her for that, and she was crazy to prolong the provocation.

But still she lingered, torn between the desire to make good her escape, and the equally strong compulsion to stay where she was. This was Nathan, her heart was pleading. Her friend; her brother; the man she had cared for for as long as she could remember. How could she desert him? She *loved* him.

Panic gripped her. That wasn't true, she thought sickly. She didn't love Nathan. She wouldn't. She couldn't. Not after what he had done to her mother; not when he must take a large proportion of the blame for the estrangement that had blighted their parents' marriage. She was just looking for an excuse not to leave, that was all. She was a fool, and a coward, and her mother had every right to despise her.

And then Nathan's eyes opened. And, before she had the chance to put any distance between them, his hand shot out and grasped her wrist. But she could see it was an automatic reaction. In those first few seconds, he'd registered only that she was standing there. He hadn't yet remembered where he was, or what he had been doing.

'India?' he said, and there was a question in his voice. 'Did I miss something?'

India swallowed. 'No, I—I was just leaving, actually.' She glanced behind her. 'It's late...'

'Yes, it is.' He blinked, and licked his lips, and as he did so his eyes changed. Maybe he'd tasted the salt on his tongue, she fretted. Whatever it was, she saw his dawning comprehension. 'So what are you doing here? Did your mother send you?'

'My mother?' India's surprise wasn't feigned. 'No, I—why would you think that?'

'Yeah. Why would I?' His tone was dry, and he pushed himself up against the back of the banquette, still retaining his hold on her wrist. Then, brushing an impatient hand over his face, he added, 'You look like a cat. Or maybe a cat burglar.'

His comment didn't deserve an answer, but she gave him one anyway. 'Well, I'm not. I...was just out for a walk, and...and I saw the lights.'

'And you were worried about me, right?'

'I didn't know it was you,' she lied, and his expression took on a sardonic slant.

'No?' His thumb massaged the network of veins at the inner side of her wrist. 'Oh, baby, you'll have to do better than that.'

His touch sent rivulets of fire up her arm, and she took a desperate breath. 'I'm not a baby, and I wish you wouldn't address me as one. And please let me go. I shouldn't have come here. I didn't mean to intrude.'

Nathan frowned. 'Now what is that supposed to mean?'

'Nothing.' She was nervously aware that she had said more than she should. 'Look, so long as you are all right, I ought to be going. We can talk in the morning.'

Nathan looked down at his hand gripping her wrist. His fingers were very brown against her pale flesh. They encircled her arm with ease, imprisoning her as surely as any manacle.

'What about?' he said, after a moment, and India was so bemused by her thoughts that she didn't immediately understand him.

'In the morning,' prompted Nathan, responding to the confusion in her eyes. 'You said we could talk in the morning, and I asked what about.'

'Oh.' India swallowed. 'I... nothing in particular.'

Nathan gave her an old-fashioned look. 'Try again.'

'I can't.' India lifted her slim shoulders. 'That is, I don't have to. There's nothing to say.'

Which wasn't what she had intended. But right now, nothing could have compelled her to tell him why she had really come here. She wasn't even sure herself any longer. Discovering Nathan was vulnerable too seemed to have swept the ground from under her.

He regarded her steadily for a moment, and she was sure he must be able to see what she was thinking. But then, tugging on her wrist, he pulled her down on to the banquette beside him.

'Tell me,' he said softly, his breath warm against her cheek, 'what do you remember about your father?'

It was the last thing she had expected, and she caught her breath. 'My father?'

'Yes, your *father*,' he repeated evenly. 'Not Aaron. Your real father.'

India hesitated. 'Well...not a lot, actually. You know he was in the army. He was away a lot. And I was only four when he died.'

'Ah.' Nathan nodded, lifting her wrist on to his thigh, and smoothing her fingers against the cloth. 'Of course.'

India gulped. His thigh was strong and powerful beneath the fine cotton of his trousers, the muscles flexing under her nervous fingers. It made her intensely aware of his maleness, and of the fact that her hand was a bare few inches from the junction of his legs.

'I just wondered how well you'd known him,' he added softly. His hand closed over hers, his long fingers sliding between hers with sensuous intent. 'How well do we ever know anybody?'

India's mouth felt dry. 'You're...talking about...your father, aren't you?' she ventured, trying to keep her mind on what he was saying, and not on what he was doing, and Nathan nodded.

'Mmm.' He gave a lazy sideways look, and her heart plunged. 'I thought I knew him—but I didn't.'

'Oh...' India looked down at their clasped hands in an effort to evade his disturbing gaze. 'Perhaps you did. He...used to talk about you, you know.'

'Did he?' Nathan looked at her bent head. 'What did he say? What an ungrateful bastard I'd proved to be?'

'No!' India's eyes jerked up to his. 'He—he was proud of you. He was. I think he would have liked to get in touch with you, but...but...'

'He didn't.'

'Couldn't! He didn't know where you were. None of us did, until... until...'

'It was too late.'

'Yes.' She sniffed. 'I'm sorry, Nathan.'

His eyes darkened. 'You're sorry for me?'

'No, not for you.' Although she was, she thought unsteadily. But Nathan wouldn't welcome her pity. 'For—for what happened. Your father dying like that. It was such a tragedy!'

'An avoidable tragedy,' said Nathan bitterly, and she made an instinctive move to free herself.

'If you're going to start that again——'

'Start what again?' Nathan had no difficulty in maintaining his hold on her hand. 'India, stop looking at me as if I were your enemy. I'm not. I'm not blaming anyone. Not even your mother—though God knows she has more to answer for than most.'

'Nathan!'

'India!' He mimicked her tone. 'You're such a loyal little thing, aren't you? Well... not so little, really. What a pity you didn't defend me as vehemently as you defend your mother.'

'Nathan...'

'What?' He looked into her eyes. 'You used to trust me. Do you remember? That time we went scuba-diving off the reef, and your tank proved to be faulty; you trusted me then. And with a hell of a lot more than your mother's reputation.'

'Oh, Nathan...'

'Mmm, I like the way you say my name.' He lifted her hand then, and carried it to his lips, brushing his tongue against the soft knuckles. 'And you taste real good.'

'I have to go...'

'You still haven't told me why you came here,' he reminded her. He turned her hand over, and bestowed a moist kiss on her palm. 'Or was this why?'

'What—I—*no*!'

Her indignation was not contrived, and Nathan gave a husky chuckle. 'Are you sure? You were pretty—hot this afternoon.'

India's lips pursed. 'How can you joke about something that was so—so...?'

'Frustrating?'

'Unforgivable,' she corrected him angrily, and his lips twisted.

'Hey, I'm not joking,' he assured her drily. 'Ask Greg. He'll tell you. It took two beers and a long, cold shower to make me feel anything like normal——'

India averted her head. 'I don't wish to hear this.'

'Don't you?' Nathan captured her chin, and brought her face up to his. 'I think that's exactly what you want to hear.'

'Well, I can't help what you think,' she retorted, concentrating on the unbuttoned neckline of his shirt to avoid looking into his eyes. 'As—as a matter of fact, I should thank you. For letting me go when you did.'

Nathan snorted. 'You little hypocrite!' he exclaimed, and, because his anger drew her attention to the pulse beating erratically in his throat, and that disturbed her, she lifted her head.

It was a mistake. She knew that immediately. She was really in no state to combat his raking gaze, particularly when his experience in these matters was so much greater than hers. Heavens, she thought, that wouldn't be difficult. Her experience was practically non-existent.

'I have to go,' she insisted stubbornly, but his eyes had softened, and she knew he was completely aware of what she really wanted.

'I think not,' he murmured, rubbing his thumb against her lower lip. 'I think you want me to kiss you, and you're terrified I'm not going to.'

'Why, you—you...'

'Flatterer,' he mocked, ignoring her outrage, and with an urgency that contradicted his own humour his mouth touched hers.

India's breath died in her throat. She knew she ought to make a fight of it, ought to push him away, but she didn't. She couldn't. That tantalising brush of his lips was so much less—yet so much more—than she had anticipated, and she made a whimpering sound of protest when it was withdrawn.

Nathan groaned then, lifting his hands to cup her face. With infinite care, he found her lips again, moving his mouth backwards and forwards, letting her feel the sensuous brush of his tongue. Her lips parted almost compulsively, and she had to suck back her disappointment when he drew back once more.

His eyes searched her face, moving swiftly from the hazy languor of her eyes to the vulnerable curve of her mouth. 'More?' he asked, his voice betraying a roughness that hadn't been there before, and India knew that this was her last chance.

'I...Nathan...'

'Are you afraid of me?' he demanded, but she shook her head.

'No....'

'Then what?'

'I don't know.'

And it was true. She no longer knew what was right or wrong, what she wanted of this man who had betrayed so much of himself. She could feel his need, knew the restraint he was exerting. Common sense told her one thing, but her mind wasn't listening. The danger she was risking was a terrible temptation.

'India...' His breath fanned her temple, and in the warm air of the cabin it was cool and moist. 'Don't—don't pretend you don't want me to touch you,' he implored her thickly. 'God knows, I've learned when a woman's willing or not.'

He would! For a moment her brain fought with the insidious desires he was arousing in her. Was this how he had seduced her mother? she wondered. Like her, had Adele been driven to the limit of her endurance?

She didn't care!

With a tremulous sigh, she admitted that what her mother might or might not have been induced to risk was no longer of any importance. Even her surroundings—the lamplit cabin with its weathered hardwood panelling, the steady lap of the water as the craft rocked at its mooring, the music and laughter distantly audible from the other vessel—had faded into insignificance. All she could see was Nathan, his hand hard and possessive on her shoulders. And when he bent his head to nuzzle her cheek, it was all academic anyway.

With a choking sound, she reached for him, clutching his neck as if she'd never let go. Her hands tangled in his hair as she tugged his mouth to hers, and this time when he kissed her he had no chance of drawing back. Even if he'd wanted to. Which she suspected he didn't, judging by the way his fingers curled around her nape, warm and insistent beneath the chunky braid of hair. And he kissed her as she had been wanting him to kiss her ever since he had left her at the beach that afternoon. Rough and tender, demanding and coaxing by turns, he bruised her mouth and eased her hunger. He wanted her. She had no doubts about that. And no matter what she had said earlier, she was past denying that she wanted him, too.

She felt the wall of the banquette at her back as his urgent kiss pinned her to the cushions. She could feel the warmth of his skin, smell the heat of his body, and the buttons of his shirt dug clear through the thin cotton of her dress. She should have worn a bra, she thought foolishly, and then was absurdly glad she hadn't when his hand slid down between them to fondle one swollen breast.

His thigh was hard against her leg, and his exploring hand caused the cloth of her dress to scrape abrasively over her taut nipples. His thumb massaged their engorged centres until she was desperate to tear the dress away, and when he bent his head to lick the cloth she moaned helplessly.

'Sweet,' he said, lifting his head, 'are you going to let me see?'

India caught her breath. 'If—if you want to.'

'I want to,' he assured her huskily, and, tipping her head up to his, he bestowed another lingering kiss on her quivering mouth.

But she was totally incapable of doing what he wanted. Even when he removed her hands from his neck and pressed them down into her lap, she could only sit there staring at him, too bemused and too embarrassed to lift the hem of the T-shirt dress.

It wasn't that she'd never undressed in front of him before. Heavens, until her mother's scathing announcement, she had thought nothing of tearing off her shirts and shorts in front of Nathan. Of course, she had usually had her bathing-suit on underneath, she acknowledged tensely. And, when she hadn't, the vest and knickers she had used to wear had been just as concealing.

But this was different, *totally* different. And she was simply not equal to the task. Even if his shirt was half open, it fell over his waistband, and since he'd opened his eyes she had purposely avoided looking there. Besides, he was probably used to this. She wasn't.

'India...'

His hand on her bare knee brought a drenching wave of heat along her thigh, and she gazed at his fingers as if she couldn't believe they could evoke such a reaction. God, she had the almost irresistible urge to open her legs and trap his hand between them, and her tongue ran helplessly over her gaping lips.

'Let me,' he added softly, and with the utmost care he eased the clinging cotton up and over her hips.

His hands slowed after exposing the lacy panties she was wearing, and India knew a momentary sense of frustration. But all he did was hook his forefinger into the flimsy briefs and tug them downwards. Then, with a smooth movement, he swept the dress over her head.

The urge to cover herself was paramount, and she wished she hadn't bound up her hair so that it offered no protection. It was worse that that afternoon on the beach, when she had at least had an excuse for her nakedness. Now she felt helpless, and exposed, and she closed her eyes instinctively, praying for deliverance.

It came in the form of Nathan's mouth caressing hers, his hands moving sensuously over her flesh. And when he drew her towards him, and she felt his hair-roughened skin against her breasts, she realised he had shed his shirt. He was still wearing his trousers. She could feel the smoothness of the cloth as he compelled her down on to the banquette and one leg slid tantalisingly between hers. But she could also feel his arousal, taut against her stomach, and she gave in to the urge to find out for herself.

'Ah—God!' he groaned when her hand found his unbuttoned waistband and slid inside. He groaned again when her fingers skated tenuously over his throbbing shaft, but she was not confident enough to tear his underwear away. Much as she wanted to find out what was beneath the cloth, her nerves got the better of her.

Besides, Nathan's fingers were probing between her legs, and she was sure she ought to stop him.

But even though her fists curled into balls, and she wanted desperately to tell him that she had never done this before, she didn't. With Nathan's tongue in her mouth, hot and wet, and demanding things of her she barely understood, there was no room for uncertainty. Besides, she was finding out things about herself that took all her concentration. The cool young woman who had found no difficulty in saying no to Steve seemed to bear no resemblance to the creature Nathan was creating. In his arms, she was fire and need, and helpless, weak abandon.

And instead of stopping him she wound her arms and legs around him, and gave herself up to the urgency of his lovemaking. If she had doubts, they were that she might disappoint him; if she ached, it was with the need to give herself to him completely.

She was hardly aware of him tearing open his trousers, tugging off his underwear, kicking them both away so that he was naked in her arms. But she was aware of the heat of him, and the strength and hardness of his maleness lying on her stomach. It was different from what she had imagined, hard, and powerful, but velvety soft to touch. And she badly wanted to touch him as he was touching her.

Between her legs, she was wet with wanting him, and when his fingers spread the damp curls she felt herself arching against him. Why didn't he do it? she fretted, half eager, half afraid of what was going to happen. But then his thumb found some sensuous core of her that quivered and ignited to his touch, and her senses spun away from her.

'Good?' he breathed, against her lips, when at last part of her reason was restored, and she nodded helplessly. Dear God, she had never expected anything like that, and she wondered if he could do it again. But now he was moving, nudging her legs wider apart, so that he could kneel between them. And when her eyes opened and she gazed up at him in some confusion, he let the hot tip of his manhood take the place of his fingers.

It felt so good—that was her first thought—and when Nathan bent his mouth to hers again she gave herself up to the wonder of his kiss. But the searing pain that followed had her whimpering and bucking beneath him, and he tore his mouth away to look down at her with incredulous eyes.

'God, India,' he muttered, 'why didn't you tell me?'

CHAPTER ELEVEN

GREG disturbed him, clattering down the stairwell with a distinct disregard for his sensibilities. 'Wake up, man,' he exclaimed, and Nathan was relieved to discover he must have got up during the night and pulled on his shorts. 'Do you know what time it is?'

Nathan didn't care. In fact, he thought, drawing up his legs and rolling into a ball, he didn't much care about anything this morning. His head ached, his mouth felt unpleasantly dry, and he had a decidedly hollow feeling in the pit of his stomach. What he really wished was that he had taken the *Wayfarer* out after India had left last night. That way he could have been sure of having some time to come to terms with what he'd done.

God, he'd fouled up, he thought bitterly. Really fouled up. Just when everything had been going so beautifully, he'd had to do something really stupid. But dammit, he was only human. And India had been so...so...

He groaned, running abrasive fingers through his hair. It wasn't as if he hadn't known how fragile their relationship was. Yet he'd still gone blundering on, destroying every thread of trust she'd ever put in him. But he'd wanted so badly for there to be no lies between them, and he'd so badly wanted to—to—to what?

He sighed, remembering. God, who would have known she was still a virgin? he wondered. She had always seemed so cool, so confident, so much in control. It was a pity a little of that control hadn't transferred itself to him.

But it hadn't, and as soon as he'd held her naked body in his arms he'd known he had to have her. All the same, as soon as he'd found out she'd never been with a man before he should have shown some sensitivity. Hell, he should have been pleased she'd never been with that guy, Whitney. It had really bugged him, seeing them together, but he had chilled him out, he thought with bitter satisfaction.

Nevertheless, it had been quite a shock discovering she was innocent, and he had reacted with predictable brashness. But, damn, he wasn't in to seducing virgins, particularly India, whom he had so much wanted to impress. *Impress*!

Well, he sure as hell hadn't impressed her then. God, as soon as he'd felt that hot, tight sheath around him he'd been three-quarters of the way there. It had only needed her quivering response for him to lose it, and he'd lain there panting over her like some premature schoolboy.

He groaned again. He should have let her go then. He should have begged her forgiveness, and prayed she wouldn't hold it against him. After all, she had insisted that she had been to blame, too. He was almost sure she had thought that was all there was to it.

But he had had to show her that it wasn't. He had had to demonstrate how macho he was by making love to her again, this time with all the skill and expertise he'd learned in a score of different beds. And the irony of it was that she had ended up by teaching him that there was more to sex than the simple gratification of the senses. With India, it had become an exercise of the mind, a spiritual thing that had fed his hunger, and made him desperate for more.

She'd been such a willing partner. God, he hadn't been able to get enough of her, and he was fairly sure she had felt the same. He'd never known a woman who was so sweet and responsive; he'd never experienced the kind of release before that he'd found in her arms.

It shouldn't have come as any surprise to him really. Deep inside, he had always known that he and India would be good together. Maybe Adele was right. Maybe he had always wanted her. Certainly he had never felt any temptation to tie himself to any other woman, and even though he hadn't known when he might see her again he had never forgotten her.

And that, he conceded, was why he had blown it. Just when she had been soft and clinging to him, when he had been firmly convinced she was beginning to trust him again, he had betrayed that trust. And why? Because he had been scared, that was why. Because he'd been afraid to trust her with what was in his heart.

Dammit! He swore silently, uncaring that Greg was staring at him with speculative eyes. He was too old to believe in fairy-tales. When she'd said she'd loved him, he hadn't believed her. And he certainly hadn't admitted he loved her too. He had made some crass remark about working it out, and he'd known, as soon as he had seen her stark face, that it hadn't been what she'd expected. God, she probably thought that was what he'd said to her mother, too. Oh, damn Adele for doing this to him. For fouling up the rest of his life.

Of course, after she'd gathered her clothes and gone he'd had a dozen excuses for what he'd done. But none of them was really valid. It was no use telling himself it was too soon, that he couldn't be sure it was what he really wanted. What *she* really wanted. Dammit, he had wanted India for a long, long time, and it wasn't doubts on that score that had caused him to turn her away.

He'd swallowed a couple more beers before exhaustion had claimed him, but his sleep had been fitful at best. In dreams he hadn't been able to hide from himself, and he had woken with the certain knowledge that what he was really afraid of was his own feelings. He had been hurt before, and he was afraid of getting hurt again.

Greg yanked back the curtains he had drawn the night before, tutting over the handful of empty cans strewn about the floor. Sunlight streamed unheeded into the cabin, and Nathan moaned, and covered his eyes against the sudden glare.

'You OK, boy?' Greg asked, coming to stand beside the banquette, and looking down at him with puzzled eyes. 'Hey, you have a party here or something?'

Nathan's mouth twisted. 'Not so's you'd notice.'

'But someone was here, right?' Greg sniffed the air. 'A lady, right?'

'What are you? Some kind of bloodhound?' grumbled Nathan, hauling himself into a sitting position, and compressing his cheeks between his hands. 'God! I feel lousy.'

'You look worse,' commented Greg, without sympathy. 'So who was it? Or is that—family business?'

Nathan's laugh was without humour. 'OK. India was here. Now are you satisfied?'

Greg frowned. 'Don't tell me: she's decided she believes you after all?'

'Do I look as if she believes me?' demanded Nathan dourly. 'Hell, Greg, I don't know what she believes. Except what a bastard I am, I guess.'

Greg looked at him for another moment, and then moved away, and began opening cupboard doors, taking out cups and coffee. 'So when are we leaving?'

'Leaving?' Nathan sounded dismayed. 'God—I don't know.'

Greg put water on to boil, and, folding his arms, leaned back against the drainer. 'You've got a meeting in New York day after tomorrow,' he reminded him. 'And you promised to attend that presentation in Dallas next Friday.'

Nathan groaned, and, resting his elbows on his knees, curled his arms over his head. The company which for so long had been the core of his existence was suddenly a burden to him, and he raised his eyes to the other man's as if desperate for his assistance.

'That bad, hmm?' remarked Greg drily, shaking his head. 'So what're you going to do?'

'I don't know.' Nathan gazed at him frustratedly. 'I think I love her, Greg. Now isn't that the pits?'

India was sitting at her father's desk when her mother charged into the room. She had been sitting there for the past hour, her head propped in her hands, staring down at its veined surface. She had been entertaining herself by wondering how many years it took to form a slab of granite of that size, but no amount of concentration could shift Nathan from her thoughts.

Nathan!

Her lips formed his name, and she closed her eyes against the pain it caused inside her. She despised him, but she *loved* him. She always would, she guessed. But after last night, she'd realised he loved no one but himself.

When she had first got back from the yacht, she'd wanted to cry. She'd let herself into her room and locked the door, convinced she was going to make a fool of herself, and wanting no spectators. Not that there had been any real chance of anyone disturbing her at four o'clock in the morning. But she'd needed the reassurance that turning a key could give.

But she hadn't cried. She'd sat down on the side of the bed, and waited for the tears to come—but they hadn't. Instead she'd felt dry, arid and curiously empty inside. As if she'd been drained of all emotion—which wasn't such a bad analogy, in the circumstances. It wasn't every evening she offered sympathy to a man and lost her virginity for her pains.

Her smile was mocking then. Dear God, she had given Nathan everything, but it hadn't been enough. Just when she had thought they were really making progress, when she had been beginning to believe they might have some chance for happiness after all, he had robbed her of that hope. With a few careless words he had reduced what had happened to a casual encounter. He had sent her on her way with barely a flicker of remorse.

Though why would he feel remorse? she'd asked herself ruefully. Heaven knew, she'd been as eager for him as he had been for her. After that initial moment when she'd dug her nails into his shoulders and stifled the scream that had risen in her, nothing else had had any meaning. She had been bewitched by his love-making, obsessed by his possession. She had never imagined—never dreamed—that he could make her feel like that. She had lost all inhibitions, lost all sense of shame. She had been honestly and totally absorbed by her emotions.

She'd realised then why he'd told her that touching and kissing weren't making love. They were just a part—a small part—of the real thing. When Nathan had possessed her, when he had thrust himself into her and given her such immense satisfaction, time had had no meaning. There had been just the driving force of pleasure, and the freedom it could give.

She had lost count of the number of times he had given her that pleasure, forgotten how many pulsating waves of freedom he'd released upon her body. All she did remember was the certainty that no one else had ever come close to making her feel so loved. Which was why it had been so devastating when he had withdrawn himself from her.

And he had withdrawn from her, mentally, if not physically, long before she had dragged on her clothes and hurried home. She'd spent hours thinking about that, wondering what had happened, where she'd gone wrong. And it all came down to one thing: in a reckless moment, she had told him she loved him. Wrapped in the throes of his passion, she'd thrown caution to the wind.

So now she was being made to regret it, she reflected bitterly. Just as she had regretted so much else in her short life. Nathan didn't want her love. He never had. But what was tearing her to pieces was the thought that she might just have been a substitute for her mother...

'Dammit, there you are, India!'

Adele's shrill voice was a potent restorative. While her mother closed the door behind her, it gave India the will to pull herself together. Dragging a file towards her, which Greg Sanders had been studying the previous afternoon, she pretended she had been working. And because Adele was so excited by what she had to relate, she let her daughter get away with it.

'Is something wrong, Mother?' India was relieved to hear her voice sounded quite normal.

'That remains to be seen.' Adele flopped down into the chair opposite, and stared at her daughter intently. 'What has Nathan told you about himself?' she demanded. 'I want to know everything he's said.'

For a moment, India wondered if Adele had found out where she had spent most of the previous night, and a trace of colour invaded her cheeks. But no. Looking at her mother, she could see no evidence of the kind of fury that would evoke in her expression, and besides, how could anyone know? Nathan had been totally discreet. He hadn't even accompanied her back to the hotel.

Forcing her thoughts from that yawning chasm, India lifted her shoulders in what she hoped was a casual gesture. 'About himself?' she echoed. 'Well, I should think you know as much as I do. All I know is, he said he'd worked in a hotel at some time. But you were there when he said it. You must remember it, too.'

'Yes, yes. But what else has he told you?' Adele was impatient. 'Did he tell you he'd been in the army? Did he tell you that was how he met this man, Greg Sanders?'

'No, Mother.' India's head was aching, and she wasn't really in the mood to indulge in question-and-answer games with Adele. If it wasn't for the fact that her absence would have caused speculation, she'd have spent the day in bed. But the last thing she wanted was for Nathan to think she cared that much about what had happened the night before.

'Are you sure?'

'Of course I'm sure.' There was an edge to India's voice now, and her mother's eyes narrowed in consideration. 'Look, Mother, if you have anything to say, why don't you come right out and say it? I—I've got some work to do, if you haven't. Until someone tells me different, I'll continue to do my job.'

'Which shouldn't be a problem,' declared Adele triumphantly, sitting back in her chair, and running her fingers over the arms. 'Kittrick's Hotel is secure, India. You have my word on it. Or rather, the word of Senator Markham. And I'd trust him further than most.'

India frowned. 'Senator Markham?' She sighed. 'What are you talking about, Mother?'

'I'm talking about Nathan, India. About that oh, so clever stepson of mine!' She chuckled. 'And we thought he might have some difficulty raising the funds to rescue Pelican Island! Darling, your brother is a millionaire! He owns a string of health resorts.'

India's jaw sagged. 'What?'

Adele clicked her tongue. 'I said, Nathan owns a string of health resorts,' she repeated impatiently. 'Don't sit there looking at me with those cow eyes, India! Haven't you got something positive to say? Like—"how clever you are, Mother". Or—"how did you find out?"'

India couldn't take it in. 'Mother...'

'Oh, very well, I'll tell you.' India had the feeling Adele intended to do so anyway, regardless of what she said. 'It was that other man that did it. Greg. Greg Sanders. You remember him, don't you?'

'Don't be silly, Mother.'

'Well—all right. Perhaps I am silly. But as soon as I saw him, I knew his face was familiar. I mean, it isn't everybody who gets their face on the cover of *Time* magazine, is it? But I remember seeing it. And when Nathan said he was his partner...well, I got to thinking, so I rang Woodie.'

'Woodie?'

'Oh, Senator Markham, then.' Adele looked a little red-faced now, and India wondered why. Though she had to say that she'd never known Adele address Senator Markham by his first name before. Not in her hearing, anyway. 'Anyway, I rang him and asked if he had heard of someone called Greg Sanders, and he knew immediately who I was talking about.'

'Nathan's partner?'

'Yes. Nathan's partner—in Sullivan's Spas! That was why Greg was on the front cover of *Time*. He'd been awarded Businessman of the Year!'

India blinked. 'I see.'

'Do you? Do you, India, *really*? I got Wood—Senator Markham to tell me all about it. It appears Nathan spent three years in the army before investing in some old fruit farm in Florida. Only, of course, he didn't use it as a fruit farm. He set up the first of his spas. Surely you've heard of Sullivan's Spas! They're all over the United States.'

'Yes. I've heard of them.'

And she had, India acknowledged dully, her head thumping like a steamhammer now. My God, no wonder Nathan thought Kittrick's Hotel was such small change. Compared to his organisation, they were chicken-feed indeed.

'Well!' Adele stared at her. 'Is that all you can say? You might show some gratitude to me for removing your worries. Nathan won't close this place. It's far too valuable to him.'

India shook her head. 'You've no guarantee of that, Mother.'

'I have. Nathan said so. Don't you remember? He said if you'd stay on as social director he'd put up the cash.'

'Yes, well . . .' India moistened her dry lips, realising how much more foolish her hopes had been in light of these revelations. Until this minute, she'd still been nurturing the thought that Nathan might discover he'd been wrong. In spite of what had happened, she'd still clung to the belief that he was still the same Nathan she'd once known. She'd hardly known that that was what she had been doing until Adele had burst into the room. But now she knew she had to do what she'd planned to do the night before. 'I—may be leaving.'

'Leaving!' Adele's shriek of disbelief was numbing. 'You can't be serious! I—I won't allow it.'

'You have nothing to do with it, Mother,' replied India flatly. 'I'm sure if you appeal to Nathan he'll let you stay on. But me—I need a change of pace. And also a change of scene.'

Adele stared at her. 'You're in love with him, aren't you?' she exclaimed incredulously. 'I suspected as much before, but . . .' She broke off abruptly. 'You're a fool!'

'I know.'

'You're not denying it, then?'

'What would be the point?' India was past caring. 'But don't worry, Mother, he doesn't love me.' Her lips twisted. 'Perhaps he's still faithful to your memory.'

'My memory?' Adele looked blank for a moment, and then her face took on a thoughtful cast. She seemed to consider what she was going to say for an inordinately long time, and India steeled herself for the disparagement she was sure was to come. But when her mother finally spoke again, it was not what she had expected to hear. 'Look, India,' she said, moving forward in her chair, and resting her arms on the edge of the desk, 'don't you think it's about time you stopped feeling so—well, so vindictive?'

'Vindictive? Me?' India gazed at her aghast.

'Yes, vindictive,' replied Adele carefully. 'I mean, if I can forgive Nathan, why can't you? He's done nothing to you, goodness knows. I'm the one who's always borne the brunt.'

Are you? India wondered what her mother would say if she told her what Nathan had done to her the night before. Would it make any difference to Adele's decision? Or would she, as India was very much afraid, regard it as just another means to an end?

She shivered, not liking the direction her thoughts were taking. When had she started to realise that Adele used people to get what she wanted? For so long she had accepted everything her mother said without question. When had she come to have doubts about her integrity?

'I—am going,' she said doggedly. 'Whatever you say, Mother, it's what I have to do.'

'Dammit, India, I won't let you!'

'You can't stop me.'

'Can't I?' Adele twisted her hands together, her long scarlet nails fluttering against her pale flesh. 'India...what if I told you I'd—exaggerated a little?'

'Exaggerated?' India blinked. 'What about?'

'Well, about Nathan, of course. What else?' Adele looked sulky.

'About his owning Sullivan's Spas, you mean?'

'Oh, don't be obtuse, India. You know how I hate it when you deliberately misunderstand me.' Adele snorted. 'I mean—about what happened that morning. The morning Aaron threw Nathan off the island.'

India trembled. 'What are you saying?'

'Didn't you hear me?' Adele was irritated.

'Yes, I heard you. But——' India got unsteadily to her feet '—I didn't believe my ears.'

'Believe them.' Adele sat back in her chair again, and crossed one trousered leg over the other. 'I may have—misunderstood what happened, that's all. I'm not saying I did,' she added hurriedly. 'But I suppose it's possible.'

CHAPTER TWELVE

NATHAN was packing his bag when someone knocked at the door of the suite. Even though he didn't want to leave, particularly now, he had let Greg persuade him that he ought to give India a little time before attempting to convince her of his feelings. She wasn't going to believe him—hell, she probably wouldn't even *listen* to him; not yet, at least. And until he had the time to explain about Sullivan's Spas, she didn't know the whole story.

Calling, 'Come in,' he continued stuffing his shaving gear into the bag. He expected it to be Greg, or maybe one of the maids, but his jaw clenched angrily when Adele slipped into the room. 'What the hell do you want?'

'Now, darling, is that any way to speak to your stepmother?' she protested lightly, but he could tell by her expression that she was not as relaxed as she would have liked to appear. 'I just want to talk to you, Nathan. That's all.'

Nathan straightened, wishing he had taken the time to get dressed before tackling his packing. After his shower he had put on the black towelling bathrobe hanging on the back of the door, and he was uncomfortably aware of his nakedness beneath the robe.

But God, he had nothing to fear from her, he told himself savagely, even though some small core of apprehension still lurked in his subconscious. This scene was too reminiscent of that other occasion, when his father had accused him of God knew what! And after reading his father's letter, he was doubly aware of her duplicity. And if India should find out...

'I think you should get out of here,' he said, keeping his voice civil with an effort. 'We've got nothing to say to one another.'

'Oh, I disagree.' Adele glanced casually around the suite, and then smiled at him again. 'This is nice, isn't it? Did you know that India had a hand in the decorations? Oh, we employed a professional firm, of course, but she had some remarkably good ideas——'

'Adele, cut it out.' Nathan pushed his fists into the pockets of his robe, and faced her grimly. 'I'm not interested in your observations concerning this suite or anything else. I just want you to go. Now. Before I call Security and have you thrown out.'

Adele's light laugh filled the room. 'Oh, Nathan! You wouldn't do that.'

'Wouldn't I?'

'No.' She took a breath. 'For one thing, it would be very hard to explain to India, wouldn't it? I mean, me here, and you just in your bathrobe.'

'You bitch!' Nathan stared at her angrily. 'If you think you're going to get away with that a second time——'

'Oh, all right.' Adele threw up her hands. 'Did I say that was what I'd come here for? No. You're jumping the gun, Nathan. I don't imagine India would be quite as gullible as her father. And, in any case, she probably wouldn't care.' She allowed a significant silence to follow these words, and then added softly, 'She says she's leaving.'

Leaving! With a superhuman effort, Nathan stopped himself from repeating the word. And although he wasn't wholly convinced that he had done a successful job of hiding his reaction, evidently he had convinced Adele.

'Well?' she demanded. 'Don't you have anything to say? Like, you're not going to let her do it?'

Nathan wasn't sure what game Adele was playing here, but he was shocked enough to let her play it. 'Why should I do that?' he asked, aware that his nails were cutting into his palms. 'I don't have any control over India's life.'

'The hell you don't!' At last he had succeeded in arousing her anger. In his experience, someone who was angry was far more likely to say what they really meant, and Adele was no exception. 'She'll do anything you want, and you know it.'

Will she? Nathan tamped down the small flame those words kindled in his stomach, and managed a careless shrug. 'I doubt it.'

'Oh, of course she will.' Adele was impatient. 'I told you years ago, the girl is infatuated with you. She always was, and I suppose she always will be. Besides, you said it was a condition in your rescue of the hotel. You can't let her leave.'

Nathan was beginning to understand. 'What you mean is, if she leaves, you'll have to do the same.'

'I didn't say that.'

'You didn't have to.' Nathan's lips twisted. 'Poor Adele! What will you do when you can't rely on your expenses being covered by the hotel? When you have to live within your means?'

Adele's face was livid. 'Oh, you'd like that, wouldn't you? You'd like to see me suffer. Well, don't fret, Nathan. It's not going to happen. You should know me better than that. I won't be leaving. Not unless you want to lose this place altogether.'

Nathan frowned. 'I'm afraid I——'

'Oh, don't use that tone with me.' Adele snorted. 'You may think you have all the answers, Nathan, but you don't. I know who you are, you see. I know all about Sullivan's Spas. You shouldn't have such a distinctive partner. I recognised his face as soon as I saw him.'

Nathan's lips thinned. Damn, he thought. Had she told India? And if she had, what new deception had Adele accused him of? He should have told India himself. God knew, he had had the chance.

'I see you understand me, Nathan. One word about our financial difficulties to the Press, and you'll have so many cancellations you won't know what to do with them. And what will happen to Kittrick's Hotel then? Your daddy's little hide-away will sink without a trace!'

Nathan sucked in his breath, and as he did so he heard another sound, like a whisper of air in the corridor outside. Greg? he wondered with some relief. Was Greg outside, listening to what was said? But the door shifted in the breeze that came through the curtains, and he guessed that was what he had heard, and not the approach of his partner.

'So what's your price?' he demanded harshly, wondering exactly how far Adele intended to go. Sure, the Press could damage them. He'd known that all along. But he wasn't going to be blackmailed. Whatever it might cost him. 'I assume you have a price?'

'Of course.' Adele was regaining her confidence. 'Don't I always? You could have stayed here all those years ago if you'd been prepared to pay it. You know that. Your father would never have known. But you were so sure he'd believe you.' She shrugged. 'And we all know how that turned out.'

'Adele——'

Nathan took an aggressive step forward, and, as if realising she was overplaying her hand, his stepmother spread her arms. 'All right, all right. Maybe you didn't want me then. Or maybe you wanted your daddy's respect more. Who knows? The truth is, you lost everything. And I don't suppose you want to risk that again.'

Nathan scowled. 'Your price, Adele. Let's hear your price. I want to know if I can afford it.'

'Oh, of course you can.' Adele clicked her tongue impatiently. 'All I want is for you to get India to stay here. She will. If you ask her. That way, I can go on——'

'Telling outrageous lies!' came a choked voice from the doorway. 'Oh, Mother! How could you? How could you be so—so gross!'

It had been the worst day of India's life. And she'd had some bad days before, she admitted, not least the day Nathan had been forced to leave his home. She had felt sick then, sick and betrayed. But nothing like the way she felt this evening, as she struggled to pack her belongings. She had so many things, so much she had gathered over the past fifteen years. This was the only home she remembered, and leaving was going to be painful.

Though not as painful as knowing she would never see Nathan again, she acknowledged hollowly. Dear God, it was a wonder he could bear to look at her, to look at *either* of them. They had taken so much from him. So much that could never be restored.

But at least she had been able to prevent her mother from doing any more damage. As soon as Adele had realised India had followed her to Nathan's room, she'd fallen apart. Faced with a daughter who not only knew the truth but had nothing to lose in using it, she had collapsed like a proverbial house of cards. The last thing she wanted was for the tabloids to publish her story. She'd read enough stories of parental abuse herself to know that someone would find India's accusations printable. And mud stuck, no matter how diligently one tried to brush it away. Besides, India suspected Adele had other things she wanted to hide—not least her association with 'Woodie' Markham.

Of course, it had been awful, having a slanging match with her mother in front of Nathan. And, although he'd attempted to intervene, she hadn't let him. God, she had never been so embarrassed as when she'd heard her mother carelessly tell him she was infatuated with him. She had nearly interrupted them then, and only the fear that there was worse to come had kept her where she was.

She didn't really know why she had followed her mother in the first place. Adele hadn't said she was going to see Nathan herself. It was just a suspicion India had had that she might take it upon herself to appeal to her stepson. Dear God, thank heaven she had acted on her suspicions. What she had heard was a blackmail attempt, no less.

She hardly remembered how she'd got her mother out of there. It had been so awful. Adele had been sobbing, wailing that it was all a mistake, that she'd only had all their best interests at heart. Of course, no one had believed her. Least of all Nathan, who, after that initial attempt to intercede, had seemed strangely indifferent to the whole proceedings.

India shuddered at the memory. Shuddered, too, at the remainder of the day, which had been spent convincing a tearful Adele that, no matter what she'd done, she was not about to desert her. For, much as she'd have liked to place the blame for what had happened eight years ago squarely on Adele's shoulders, she couldn't ignore her own complicity in the event. She had been so quick to judge Nathan, so eager to take her mother's word over that of a friend who had never betrayed her.

She didn't know how Nathan had spent the day. As far as she knew, he could have left the island. It certainly looked as if he had been packing when she'd barged into his suite. She had seen the bag on the chest behind him, noticed it even though she had thought all her attention had been concentrated on her mother. But then she'd noticed that Nathan was just wearing a bathrobe, too, his hair slick against his neck, and gleaming from his shower.

She made a sound of despair. She doubted she could be anywhere near Nathan without noticing him. She didn't even have to see him to know he was there. It was a psychological thing, a feeling, an intangible awareness of the man she loved.

The suitcase was packed, and, snapping the catches, she hoisted it off the bed and on to the floor. Then, adjusting her balance, she heaved it to the door. That made two, she thought, viewing her efforts without enthusiasm. It was going to take ages at this rate. Perhaps she ought to get someone to help her.

But who? Her lips twisted. Her mother? She thought not. Adele had enough packing of her own to do. Not that India really believed that that was what Adele was doing. If she knew her mother, she'd wait until India had completed her packing, and then get her daughter to do hers for her. She was probably sitting in her room at this moment, smoking a cigarette, and consoling herself with gin and tonics. Adele liked gin and tonic—except when she was worrying about what it might do to her skin. Adele worried about her skin. But not tonight, thought India drily. Even her mother must realise she had more important things to worry about than whether she'd acquired a few more wrinkles.

The cases looked ugly, standing by the door. They didn't go with the green and gold luxury of the room. They were spoiling what was, conceivably, the last night she might spend in these apartments. The least she could do was put them next door, somewhere where she couldn't see them.

Heaving a sigh, she took hold of one of the suitcases, and dragged it through the lamplit beauty of her sitting-room. But the case offended her no less in these surroundings either. To hell with it, she thought, she'd put them in the corridor. It wasn't as if anyone was likely to walk off with them. And even if someone did, she didn't particularly care.

She opened the door, and was struggling to heave the heavy suitcase over the threshold when she saw the tan loafers. They were set squarely outside her door, and her eyes travelled up over navy silk trousers, and a tan silk shirt, opened at the neck to reveal the brown skin of his throat.

Nathan's throat, she acknowledged tightly, aware of who it was long before her eyes reached the unsmiling harshness of his face. It was strange that she had just been thinking about the affinity they shared, she reflected tensely. Or perhaps it was just a one-sided thing. He certainly didn't look as if he was in affinity with her at the moment.

He didn't say anything, however, and it was left to her to make the first overture. 'Oh, hello,' she said, scolding herself for sounding as if she had nothing more important on her mind than the need to respect the formalities. 'I'm sorry. I didn't hear you.' Or I'd have made sure I was wearing something better than shorts and an outsize T-shirt, she added, for her ears only.

'I didn't knock,' he essayed drily, and she wondered if she had only imagined the faint humour in his voice. 'Can I come in, anyway? I need to talk to you.'

'I . . .' India glanced behind her. 'I thought you'd left.'

'As you can see, I haven't.'

'But you are leaving?'

'Does it matter?' He looked up and down the corridor irritably. 'Look, do you want to attract attention? All I want is a few minutes of your time. Now do I have it?'

India swallowed and stood back, holding on to the door. 'I suppose so.'

'Great.' He stepped inside. 'I assume that you're alone.'

India hesitated, and then closed the door and leant back against it. 'As you can see,' she conceded, using his words, 'I—I was just packing.' She lifted her shoulders. 'There's such a lot to do.'

'Then don't do it.'

India caught her lower lip between her teeth. 'I—prefer to. I don't like other people——'

'I meant—don't go,' said Nathan harshly. He stood facing her across the silky Chinese carpet, his hands pressed insistently to the front of his thighs. 'You don't have to leave, India. And this has nothing to with your mother. This is your home, dammit. If you want to stay, stay!'

India was glad of the panels of the door at her back. 'You don't mean that.'

'I do mean it.'

She licked her lips. 'You don't owe us anything,' she protested.

'Did I say I did?' His hands curled into balls and he let them hang at his sides. 'God, India, this is so hard for me! Don't make it any harder. I want you to stay, do you understand me? I want you to do what you want.'

'What I want?'

'Yeah. What you want.' He expelled his breath, and glanced frustratedly around him. 'Is there anything to drink around here?'

India started away from the door. 'I've got Coke...'

'That should do it.'

'Or I could go and get you a beer.'

'*You* go and get me a beer?' he echoed. 'Don't be an idiot! You don't have to run around after me. Hell, Coke will be great. So long as it's not one of those diet sodas.'

'It's not.'

India hurried past him, trying to keep her mind on one thing at a time. But her mind was obsessed with the reasons why Nathan had come here, and, although she knew she was crazy, his offer was too tempting to dismiss out of hand.

The tiny cold-box concealed inside a carved ebony cabinet was always full of cold drinks. It was the facsimile of the small fridges found in all the guest bedrooms. Only in their case they were filled with tonics and sodas, a supplement to the complimentary decanters of Scotch and sherry that were a popular feature of the hotel. India's, however, contained only Perrier and Coke, and she had no difficulty in extracting a can and handing it to him.

Her fingers brushed his in passing, but she tried not to think about how cool they felt, or to remember that the night before they had been caressing her willing flesh. Whatever Nathan had to say to her could only be complicated by her reactions to him, and she had to keep the knowledge of his rejection of her in the forefront of her mind.

Nathan tore off the tab, and swallowed half the contents of the can in a single gulp, and then, wiping his mouth on the back of his hand, he gave her a grateful look. 'Thanks.'

India shifted a little awkwardly. 'My pleasure,' she replied, and then, realising how that might sound, she added hastily, 'It's very hot.'

'Isn't it?' Nathan looked down at the can, and then set it down on the top of the cabinet. 'And I'm not talking about the weather.'

India stifled a gasp. 'I—I don't know what you mean.'

'Don't you?' His eyes searched her face. 'Why don't I believe you?'

India tucked her fingers under her arms. 'I don't know.'

'Do you think it's because I'm not used to hearing the truth from your side of the family?' he suggested mildly, and India's brief spurt of optimism fled.

'Could—could be,' she agreed, seeking the safety of her previous position beside the door. 'But—but if you feel like that, I don't know why you've asked me to stay on. If you feel any responsibility towards Adele, don't. I can look after both of us.'

Nathan's expression hardened. 'I don't feel any responsibility for Adele,' he said. 'I don't feel anything for Adele, period. It's you I'm concerned about. Haven't you grasped that yet?'

His tone was hardly encouraging, and India could feel the faint stirrings of resentment in her stomach. Dammit, did he have to make it sound as if she were some kind of mental defective? She'd got the picture. He'd made his position very clear last night.

'Well,' she said, choosing her words with care, 'I'm sure I ought to be flattered——'

'*India*!'

'—that you feel some responsibility for me, but it's really not necessary. And if what you really mean is that you're suffering some sense of duty for what happened last night——'

But she didn't get a chance to finish. With a muffled oath, Nathan closed the gap between them, backing her up against the door, and stifling her words with his mouth.

'God,' he groaned at last, when he released her lips to seek the scented hollow of her shoulder. 'I guess I deserved to hear that, but I think we deserve this more.'

India's head was swimming, but she strove to hang on to her sanity. 'You don't have to do this, Nathan,' she insisted. 'Just because Adele told you how I... how I felt about you, you don't have to pretend you feel the same. You were leaving. I saw you'd been packing your bag. Oh, please, Nathan, let me go. This isn't going to work.'

'It seems to be working pretty good to me,' retorted Nathan mildly, and, feeling the muscled ridge of his pelvis hard against her stomach, India at least had the satisfaction of knowing he wasn't lying. But arousing him and loving him were two entirely different things. 'Baby, listen to me. I've waited all day for you to put me out of my misery.'

'Your misery?' India was confused.

'Yes, my misery,' agreed Nathan huskily. 'India, I need to know that you forgive me. For causing this rift between you and your mother.'

India tipped back her head to look at him. 'That's crazy!'

'Is it?' Nathan traced the outline of one arching brow with his finger. 'Sweetheart, that woman's caused so much grief between us. I wouldn't put it past her to try and turn you against me even now.'

'Oh, Nathan...' India's eyes were moist.

'Does that mean you forgive me?'

She shook her head. 'There's nothing to forgive.'

'Not even what I did last night?' he reminded her softly, and then groaned as her knee almost found its target.

'I knew it,' she cried, gazing at him with tears standing in her eyes now. 'I knew that was why you were really here. You were going away. Don't try to deny it. So what changed your mind? Or don't I want to know?'

Nathan backed off, but he didn't let her get away from him. He imprisoned her between his outstretched arms, and she fidgeted beneath his penetrating gaze.

'OK,' he conceded with a sigh. 'I was leaving. You're right. I was packing my bags and getting the hell out of here while I had the chance. But not because I didn't care about you. You should know better than that. It was because I was too damn scared to tell you how I felt.'

India tried to drag her eyes away from his, but although she moved her head he wouldn't let her. Instead, she stayed, riveted by his stare, feeling every inch of flesh prickling in protest.

'I... don't... believe... you.'

'Why not?'

She shook her head. 'You're not scared of anything.'

'Oh, aren't I?' Nathan's mouth twisted. 'You'd be surprised.'

She sighed. 'Don't do this,' she said. 'Don't make a fool of me, Nathan. All right. I still love you. Is that what you wanted to hear?'

'I want to hear a hell of a lot more than that,' he said thickly, and, ignoring the way she flinched away from him, he ran his tongue around the delicate spiral of her ear. 'Like—you'll marry me, for instance. And you won't ask your mother to be your matron of honour!'

'Don't!' India doubled under his arm then, and put the width of the room between them. Then, wringing her hands, she cried, 'You don't have to do this, Nathan. It's... it's kind of you, and I... I do appreciate your loyalty, but——'

Nathan turned, resting his shoulders against the door, his chin dipping wearily to his chest. 'How many more times?' he demanded. 'I'm not doing this for you, India. I'm doing it for me. I love you, dammit. I guess I always have. But when you get hurt it takes you a hell of a long time before you put your trust in anyone again!'

India trembled. 'All right. You care about me. But you don't have to marry me.'

'Oh, yes, I do.' Nathan pushed himself away from the door, and this time she didn't back away when he came towards her. 'I'm not taking any chances as far as you're concerned. You're going to be my wife, and I won't ever let you forget it!'

* * *

Hours later, India stirred to find Nathan playing sensuously with her hair. 'At least I know I'm the only person who can prove you're really a redhead,' he teased softly, spreading it across one rosy nipple, and she pulled an indignant face.

'You sound smug.'

'I am.' He grinned. 'I never thought about it before, but it really makes me feel good. I used to think about you getting married and having children. Now I know why it felt like a kick in the—well, gut.'

India expelled her breath on a tremulous sigh. 'Are you sure this is what you want?'

He pulled an old-fashioned face. 'I'm sure.'

'But... you must have met other women...'

'Yes.'

'And... and made love to other women...'

'Had sex, anyway,' he amended agreeably.

'Well, then, why...?'

'Why you?' She nodded. 'Because that's what all those other women were. Just—sex. Nothing else. With you it's different. Don't ask me why. I just knew, as soon as I touched you, you... well——' he drew her hand down to his body '—you're the one.'

'Oh, Nathan!'

'Yeah. Corny, isn't it?' He grimaced. 'But those other women, they didn't mean a thing. Last night—last night was just the culmination of feelings I've been fighting ever since I got back to the island. I told myself I couldn't love someone who didn't even trust me. But I couldn't leave you alone, baby. And that's when I knew I was in serious, serious trouble.'

India sniffed. 'All right. You've convinced me. I'll stay.'

'Stay?' Nathan looked blank now, and she fumbled for the right words.

'Here,' she said. 'On the island. I'll do whatever you want me to do. Just tell me what it is.'

'Oh, God!' Nathan rolled until he was lying half over her, one leg wedged comfortably between hers. 'Sweetheart, I forgot to tell you; I live in New York. Do you think you can stand to do that?'

The little jet banked over the island, and India turned to look at Nathan lounging in the seat beside her.

'We're almost there,' she said, running a rueful hand over the swelling in her belly. 'It's just as well. I think your son is getting impatient.'

Nathan grinned, leaning over her, and passing a possessive hand over the mound of her stomach, and down to the apex of her legs. 'What would you say if I told you his father is getting impatient too?' he murmured. 'Don't forget, I've been marooned in British Columbia for the past week. It seems forever since I've seen you. I hope your mother doesn't fuss. I want you to myself.'

India stretched with unknowing sensuality. 'We'll have the nights,' she said, enjoying his hungry appraisal. 'Darling, don't look at me like that. I'm sure Elena thinks you're crazy.'

'To hell with what Elena thinks,' he retorted, without giving the stewardess even half a glance. 'I'm with my wife, and I'll look at her how I like.'

India smiled, and then, because Nathan's stare was making her restless, she turned her gaze back to the window. Already she could see the walls of the new extension, towering beside the marina. In twelve months Nathan and Greg had accomplished so much, and they were here now to celebrate the hotel's reopening.

'Anyway, at least Greg will be there to run interference,' Nathan added now, lifting his wife's fall of hair, and bestowing a moist kiss on her nape. 'Last time I spoke with him, he said he and Adele were getting along just fine. You know, he may be just what your mother needs. Someone who won't play her games, but who she finds quite a challenge.'

India chuckled. 'You could be right. Though I can't say I envy him. Still, learning she's going to be a grandmother has sort of clipped her wings.'

'Mmm.' Nathan nodded, thinking of the letter he had destroyed soon after they were married. He had thought long and hard about Aaron's letter, but he had finally decided India didn't deserve to bear that burden too.

Besides, Aaron was dead. As he had said, his sins, and Adele's, had died with him. Nathan had the woman he loved. He could afford to be generous.

India, sensing her husband's sudden preoccupation, turned to him curiously. 'Is anything wrong?'

'No.' Nathan shook his head, and meant it. 'I was just thinking how much I love you, that's all. Remind me to tell you again later.'

And she did.

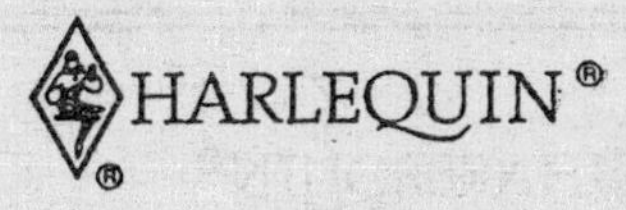

WEDDING INVITATION
Marisa Carroll

Brent Powell is marrying Jacqui Bertrand, and the whole town of Eternity is in on the plans. This is to be the first wedding orchestrated by the newly formed community co-op, Weddings, Inc., and no detail is being overlooked.

Except perhaps a couple of trivialities. The bride is no longer speaking to the groom, his mother is less than thrilled with her, and her kids want nothing to do with *him*.

WEDDING INVITATION, available inJune from Superromance, is the first book in Harlequin's exciting new cross-line series, **WEDDINGS, INC.** Be sure to look for the second book, **EXPECTATIONS,** by Shannon Waverly (Harlequin Romance #3319), coming in July.

INDULGE A LITTLE 6947 SWEEPSTAKES
NO PURCHASE NECESSARY

HERE'S HOW THE SWEEPSTAKES WORKS:
The Harlequin Reader Service shipments for January, February and March 1994 will contain, respectively, coupons for entry into three prize drawings: a trip for two to San Francisco, an Alaskan cruise for two and a trip for two to Hawaii. To be eligible for any drawing using an Entry Coupon, simply complete and mail according to directions.

There is no obligation to continue as a Reader Service subscriber to enter and be eligible for any prize drawing. You may also enter any drawing by hand printing your name and address on a 3" x 5" card and the destination of the prize you wish that entry to be considered for (i.e., San Francisco trip, Alaskan cruise or Hawaiian trip). Send your 3" x 5" entries to: Indulge a Little 6947 Sweepstakes, c/o Prize Destination you wish that entry to be considered for, P.O. Box 1315, Buffalo, NY 14269-1315, U.S.A. or Indulge a Little 6947 Sweepstakes, P.O. Box 610, Fort Erie, Ontario L2A 5X3, Canada.

To be eligible for the San Francisco trip, entries must be received by 4/30/94; for the Alaskan cruise, 5/31/94; and the Hawaiian trip, 6/30/94. No responsibility is assumed for lost, late or misdirected mail. Sweepstakes open to residents of the U.S. (except Puerto Rico) and Canada, 18 years of age or older. All applicable laws and regulations apply. Sweepstakes void wherever prohibited.

For a copy of the Official Rules, send a self-addressed, stamped envelope (WA residents need not affix return postage) to: Indulge a Little 6947 Rules, P.O. Box 4631, Blair, NE 68009, U.S.A.

INDR93

INDULGE A LITTLE 6947 SWEEPSTAKES
NO PURCHASE NECESSARY

HERE'S HOW THE SWEEPSTAKES WORKS:
The Harlequin Reader Service shipments for January, February and March 1994 will contain, respectively, coupons for entry into three prize drawings: a trip for two to San Francisco, an Alaskan cruise for two and a trip for two to Hawaii. To be eligible for any drawing using an Entry Coupon, simply complete and mail according to directions.

There is no obligation to continue as a Reader Service subscriber to enter and be eligible for any prize drawing. You may also enter any drawing by hand printing your name and address on a 3" x 5" card and the destination of the prize you wish that entry to be considered for (i.e., San Francisco trip, Alaskan cruise or Hawaiian trip). Send your 3" x 5" entries to: Indulge a Little 6947 Sweepstakes, c/o Prize Destination you wish that entry to be considered for, P.O. Box 1315, Buffalo, NY 14269-1315, U.S.A. or Indulge a Little 6947 Sweepstakes, P.O. Box 610, Fort Erie, Ontario L2A 5X3, Canada.

To be eligible for the San Francisco trip, entries must be received by 4/30/94; for the Alaskan cruise, 5/31/94; and the Hawaiian trip, 6/30/94. No responsibility is assumed for lost, late or misdirected mail. Sweepstakes open to residents of the U.S. (except Puerto Rico) and Canada, 18 years of age or older. All applicable laws and regulations apply. Sweepstakes void wherever prohibited.

For a copy of the Official Rules, send a self-addressed, stamped envelope (WA residents need not affix return postage) to: Indulge a Little 6947 Rules, P.O. Box 4631, Blair, NE 68009, U.S.A.

INDR93

INDULGE A LITTLE
SWEEPSTAKES

OFFICIAL ENTRY COUPON

This entry must be received by: APRIL 30, 1994
This month's winner will be notified by: MAY 15, 1994
Trip must be taken between: JUNE 30, 1994-JUNE 30, 1995

YES, I want to win the San Francisco vacation for two. I understand that the prize includes round-trip airfare, first-class hotel, rental car and pocket money as revealed on the "wallet" scratch-off card.

Name____________________

Address ______________ Apt. ________

City____________________

State/Prov.__________ Zip/Postal Code________

Daytime phone number__________________
(Area Code)

Account #____________________

Return entries with invoice in envelope provided. Each book in this shipment has two entry coupons—and the more coupons you enter, the better your chances of winning!

 MONTH1

INDULGE A LITTLE
SWEEPSTAKES

OFFICIAL ENTRY COUPON

This entry must be received by: APRIL 30, 1994
This month's winner will be notified by: MAY 15, 1994
Trip must be taken between: JUNE 30, 1994-JUNE 30, 1995

YES, I want to win the San Francisco vacation for two. I understand that the prize includes round-trip airfare, first-class hotel, rental car and pocket money as revealed on the "wallet" scratch-off card.

Name____________________

Address ______________ Apt. ________

City____________________

State/Prov.__________ Zip/Postal Code________

Daytime phone number__________________
(Area Code)

Account #____________________

Return entries with invoice in envelope provided. Each book in this shipment has two entry coupons—and the more coupons you enter, the better your chances of winning!

© 1993 HARLEQUIN ENTERPRISES LTD. MONTH1